"How about a walk on the beach..." he
asked her.

Christine nodded enthusiastically.

"On one condition," he told her. "We stay dry
this time."

She smiled. "You've got a deal."

He gave her one of his jackets to slip into, and
she giggled over the way it hung to her knees.
"It'll keep you warm," he promised, throwing
his arm around her shoulders as they started
off down the beach.

The night was shrouded in fog. The surf was
only a few feet away, but they couldn't see it
through the gauzy mist. It seemed they were the
only two people in the world.

After a while, Bear stopped. "We're here."

She looked around. They were caught in a
bank of fog. "How can you tell?"

"Trust me."

She stood close and looked into his eyes. "I do
trust you."

His dark gaze dropped to her mouth, and the
look was intimate, tactile. "I wonder," he said
softly, "what would happen if I . . ." He lowered his head to hers, to nuzzle, to smell the
sweetness of her skin and feel the softness of
her face next to his. He offered a tenderness he
hadn't known was his to give.

She stepped into his embrace, seeking the
warmth, the intimacy. If he'd demanded more
of her, she could have rebelled, but his gentleness was her undoing. . . .

WHAT ARE *LOVESWEPT* ROMANCES?

They are stories of true romance and touching emotion. We believe those two very important ingredients are constants in our highly sensual and very believable stories in the *LOVESWEPT* line. Our goal is to give you, the reader, stories of consistently high quality that may sometimes make you laugh, sometimes make you cry, but are always fresh and creative and contain many delightful surprises within their pages.

Most romance fans read an enormous number of books. Those they truly love, they keep. Others may be traded with friends and soon forgotten. We hope that each *LOVESWEPT* romance will be a treasure—a "keeper." We will always try to publish

LOVE STORIES YOU'LL NEVER FORGET
BY AUTHORS YOU'LL ALWAYS REMEMBER

The Editors

Loveswept ® 565

Lori Copeland
Built to Last

BANTAM BOOKS
NEW YORK · TORONTO · LONDON · SYDNEY · AUCKLAND

BUILT TO LAST

A Bantam Book / September 1992

If you would be interested in receiving protective vinyl
covers for your Loveswept books, please write to this address
for information:

Loveswept
Bantam Books
P.O. Box 985
Hicksville, NY 11802

ISBN 0-553-44094-2

Published simultaneously in the United States and Canada

PRINTED IN THE UNITED STATES OF AMERICA

OPM   0 9 8 7 6 5 4 3 2 1

One

"Oh, brother," Christine murmured as she pulled into the gravel driveway. "What have I gotten myself into this time?"

Switching off the motor, she gazed at the sagging roof and broken windows of the old two-story frame house she'd volunteered her Saturday to help renovate.

"Ah, it'll be fun," she told herself, repeating the line she was using to recruit other young professionals to donate their free time to a project she believed in: Converting abandoned houses into affordable homes for low-income families.

Shrugging off her momentary regret, she tossed her keys into her handbag, then picked her way over the gaping holes in the wooden porch. She felt her heartbeat speed up as it always did just before she tackled a new project. Whether polishing brass or waxing her car, she enjoyed watching a faint glow bloom to a deep shine before her eyes, knowing that her effort had made the difference. Physical work was always a welcome release after a work week that kept her behind a desk all day and a telephone that seemed like another appendage of her body.

As a supervisor in an electronics firm, she arranged for materials to arrive just in time for assembly. Since her contribution was only the first step in the process, she missed the thrill of accomplishment that came from seeing a project through from beginning to end.

"Hello? Anybody home?" she called at the open door, feeling a little foolish. The ramshackle old house at the outskirts of Santa Cruz had been deserted long before the last earthquake had rearranged its parts. Opening the creaky screen door, she stepped inside.

She stood for a moment, waiting for her eyes to adjust to the dim interior. Even the California sunshine couldn't pierce the cloud of dust layering the air. When she could distinguish gray shapes and dark outlines, she crossed the room, dodging boards and boxes, recognizing some of the labels from lumberyards she'd coaxed into donating supplies.

She was hanging her shoulder bag over a doorknob when she heard a rustle. Her body tensed as her eyes scanned the debris strewn over the floor. Maybe there were rats. She hadn't bargained for that.

"About time you showed up."

Christine jerked around to face the source of the deep masculine rumble. Across the room stood a huge man, his shoulders nearly spanning the doorway. She could discern only his outline.

Thick, tousled hair framed his head like a mane. Her glance jumped down his muscled arms to linger on the hammer hanging loosely from his hand. As if he could sense her alarm, he twirled the hammer deftly in his fingers and let it drop into the denim loop at his hips. The long handle bounced twice before settling against his thigh. Her glance dropped down his widespread legs, two long columns of muscle, to his scuffed work boots.

"Hello?" she answered lamely. When he took a step toward her, she fought the urge to flee.

"Weren't you supposed to show up an hour ago?"

"Who are you?"

"Bear Malone."

She swallowed the swell of panic rising in her throat. Bear Malone was the man she'd been told to report to. "I am on time." Punctuality was something she took pride in.

He took a few strides toward her, and she could see that his dark hair was flecked with wood chips and plaster. When he stopped, his presence dominated the room. He glanced over his shoulder through the broken window and gave her red BMW a quick assessment. His heavy brows lowered in a scowl. "You the Brighton woman?"

"Yes, Christine Brighton from ElectroFirst Incorporated."

He nodded. "They said you'd be here an hour ago. I could've used a hand with that drywall."

She straightened. "I was told to be here at nine."

"What time is it now?"

She glanced at the sports watch she wore on weekends. "It's five till nine." His attitude was beginning to annoy her. "I take it you don't wear a watch?"

"Don't need one. It'd only get in my way." He looked at her then, his glance flicking up and down.

She could guess what he was thinking. She was tall but small-boned, and most people assumed she wasn't half as strong as she was.

When she spoke, her words sounded like ice cubes clinking in a glass. "Perhaps you should check the time *before* you accuse someone of being late."

Bear Malone shifted his gaze back to her car, glistening like a ruby under the September sun. With the last house he'd renovated, he'd done pretty much all the work although he'd had a crew of volunteers. They were all the same type as Christine Brighton, and Bear expected her to act as they did: Hang around for an hour just to rack up a few brownie points that would impress the boss.

He shrugged. "Whatever." Turning, he headed back toward the doorway. She followed in his wake, catching the last of his mumblings: "Ask for a work crew, and what do you get—a damn yuppie."

With a terse nod and a few gestures, he instructed her to collect the hunks of drywall and wood that were scattered around the floor. Obviously, he didn't think she was qualified for anything more imaginative. She found an empty box, filled it, and carried it out to the back. Annoyed by his abrupt dismissal, she tossed the trash onto the heap with great relish, pretending that she was flinging it at the rude, arrogant brute inside. It irked her that his disapproving attitude could make her feel defensive and more than a little guilty about having a few nice things.

"Bear Malone," she muttered, chucking scraps onto the pile. "Well, at least your name suits you: Big as a bear and twice as cranky."

After half a dozen trips, the edges of her anger had cooled. She hadn't exchanged a word with Bear in the past half hour, and now she glanced at him over her shoulder. He seemed totally absorbed in his task, pounding on an obstinate wall that refused to come down. Even though he'd torn off most of the drywall and cut the studs with a chain saw, the wall stood its ground.

"Damn thing won't budge," he muttered.

Christine paused to watch him take turns with a pry bar and then a sledgehammer. The supports trembled but refused to buckle. She could see that what he needed was for someone to apply leverage with the pry bar at one end while he did some persuading with the sledge at the other.

Without being asked, she picked up the heavy pry bar and wedged it into a cut he'd made in one of the supports. Bear glanced at her as he paused for a moment.

She nodded at the sledge in his grip. "Well, give it another lick."

He looked as though he was on the verge of actually laughing when he seemed to think better of it. Instead, he gave a brief nod and fixed his gaze on the wall. Drawing a deep breath, he lifted the sledge with a slow, deliberate roll of his shoulders. The timbers splintered on impact.

Instinctively, Christine tightened her grip on the pry bar as Bear glanced at her. "Use your legs, not your back."

She nodded and gripped the bar tighter. A couple more solid hits from the sledge and the studs began to snap.

When the wall gave way, so did the resistance against her pry bar. Caught off guard, Christine pitched forward but a pair of strong hands reached out to catch her. Bear snagged her waist and held her suspended in air long enough for her to regain her balance.

"Thanks," she murmured as he settled her back on her feet.

"You hurt yourself?"

"No." She took a step back to break the contact.

She was obviously flustered, and Bear decided that he liked her that way, her brown eyes huge and round, her creamy skin heightened by a pink flush, her auburn waves brushing her shoulders as she looked up at him. She was so alive . . . and vulnerable, like a bird perched on the immediate decision to stay or fly.

"You looked for a minute like you were going to faint," he said.

"I'm not going to faint." Her voice sounded harsher than she'd intended. "I'm stronger than I look."

For some reason, she felt uncomfortable under his scrutiny. He wasn't the sort to look at a woman with covert glances. He was staring at her openly now as if trying to figure out what made her tick. Brushing her hands off on her jeans, she glanced where the wall had stood, hoping to distract him. "By the way, why did we tear it down?"

"This was the living room"—he nodded at the area beyond where the wall lay in rubble—"and that was a parlor. Nowadays one large family room will serve better."

She glanced at the ceiling. "Is there enough support?"

His gaze followed hers. "I checked it out first. That beam is sturdy enough to support a lot of weight."

"I hope you're right." Though she sounded doubtful, she suspected that if Bear Malone said something was a certain way, she could count on it.

Glancing up, she caught him looking at her again. She was a woman who could effectively ignore a man's stare if she chose, but this man's look was so penetrating that it seemed to pierce her soul.

She did something unlike her; she broke eye contact. She was aware that her fingers were trembling slightly as she tucked them into her hip pockets. To her dismay, his gaze seemed to catch that too.

"You'd better sit down for a while. You still look shaky."

She shrugged, trying not to let him see that his observation was making her all the more flustered. "I'm okay, just a little hungry. It's time for my midmorning snack."

She didn't like the way he made her feel awkward and self-conscious. She prized being in control, on the job and off.

She headed for her handbag and dug out a nutrition bar. To her dismay, Bear followed her, strolling idly along, scooping up his thermos bottle and tucking it under his arm. Leaning against the doorjamb, he poured a cup of steaming coffee as he watched her. The aroma overrode the smell of fresh-cut lumber. With a lifted brow, he reached toward her to offer his cup.

"No, thanks." She shook her head. "Never touch the stuff."

His brows lifted in surprise. "How do you wake up mornings?"

"I drink mineral water and have one of these." She held up the foil-wrapped bar.

"What in the hell is that?"

She nodded. "A nutrition bar."

She could tell he had never been near one.

"It's full of vitamins and minerals."

His gaze drifted through the front windows. "Looks like your BMW has a little company."

There was a touch of sarcasm in his voice, but she chose to ignore it as she looked out the window to see if someone was tinkering with her car. Her eyes closed briefly when she saw that a yellow Ferrari had pulled into the driveway.

"Excuse me," she said, hoping that Bear would take the hint and wander off discreetly. "I know him."

Bear's eyes moved back to the Ferrari. "Figures."

As she headed toward the door, she was aware that he was still lounging in the doorway sipping his coffee, in no hurry to grant her any privacy with her visitor.

"Hi, Percy," she said evenly, standing behind the torn screen door.

"Yo, babe." The young man tossed his head, sending his short curtain of dark hair swinging around his head. When she didn't immediately open the screen door, he added, "Aren't you going to invite me in?"

Christine sent a sidelong glance in Bear's direction as she pushed open the door. "Sure, but it's a little messy in here."

Percy stepped over the threshold and tossed the room and Bear Malone a cursory glance. Looking down, he carefully set his feet so his shiny penny Loafers wouldn't get scuffed. "So . . . you about finished here?"

"No." For some reason she was acutely aware that Bear was listening to every word. "Does it look done to you?"

Percy's gaze swung to the cracked ceiling, the crumbling walls, and the curling linoleum floor. "Looks hopeless to me."

The sudden distaste in Percy's eyes filled Christine with stubborn determination. "Well, you'll have to come back when it's finished. It'll look a lot different then."

Percy's expression conveyed that such concerns were beneath him. "About lunch, babe, there's a great little seafood place not twenty minutes from here." He consulted his gold Rolex. "If we leave now, I think we'll just make the reservation. I had the damnedest time finding this place. If it hadn't been for your red BMW—"

"I can't go today," Christine interrupted. "I told you that yesterday."

At the rebuff, Percy's eyes pivoted in Bear's direction; Christine's involuntarily followed. Sure enough, Bear Malone was all ears. In fact, he was making no pretense of his listening in. His gaze shifted back and forth between the two as if he were watching a tennis match.

"Well," Percy said, "I thought I'd just drop by on the off chance you'd had enough." He glanced around the room again. "I really can't see how a few hours for lunch could make much difference."

"I'm sorry, but I really can't spare the time."

Percy's condescending attitude toward her project had bugged her all week. She'd politely accepted his refusal to join her when she'd tried to recruit his help for today. Now his unannounced visit was making her uncomfortable . . . especially in the presence of Bear Malone, who was watching their exchange with the detached curiosity of one who'd tuned into a soap opera for the first time.

Christine glared at Bear and blinked a few

times, hoping he'd take the hint and amble into the next room. In response, Bear casually pushed away from the doorway.

Oh, good, he's going to move on, Christine thought until she saw him step astride a sawhorse and lean back to pour himself another cup of coffee. When his eyes met hers, she saw the glint of challenge. As he brought the steaming cup to his lips, he had the gall to lift it ever so slightly in a silent salute.

She exhaled in a huff. "Come on, Percy. Let's step outside."

She marched down the steps with Percy following behind. "The nerve of that man," she said when they were out of earshot.

"What did you expect from a muscle-bound carpenter? Manners? Scrub the project, babe. Let's do lunch."

"I can't leave now. That's probably what he expects me to do."

"Who cares what he thinks?" Percy's voice lifted an octave. "That overgrown throwback to the sixties—what does he know, anyway?"

Christine sighed. "He knows how to restore houses. And he's good at what he knows. And right now, he's the only volunteer we have who understands all phases of renovation."

"How do you know what he is? Has anybody checked under all that hair?"

When he reached for her arm, she could see that besides a new haircut and style, he'd gotten a fresh manicure as well.

"Percy, I'm sorry, but I can't go with you."

"Suit yourself." There was more than a hint of pout in his voice as he turned and walked to his car. A moment later the Ferrari spit gravel as he backed out of the driveway.

Christine shook her head as she watched him leave. Percy was twenty-four, two years younger than she, and a new management trainee at ElectroFirst. At times like this, he seemed much younger than his years. Christine found herself wondering why she even put up with him.

Perhaps because from the first moment they'd met he was easy to be with. Unlike men like Bear Malone, Percy did not overwhelm her or tie her nerves in a knot. And he never made her feel that she had to justify her lifestyle.

Christine took pride in being open-minded. She had never tried to change anyone, and she never would. It just wasn't her style. She suspected that Bear Malone tended to make snap judgments.

Christine reentered the house, and found Bear in the next room, examining the jagged wooden remnants that hadn't toppled with the rest of the wall. As he tested the strength of a stubborn snag where once a wall stud had stood, he neither spoke nor looked at her.

She took a step forward, but halted when he said firmly, "Stay put and cover your eyes with your hands."

"Yes, master," she replied before she could quash the impulse.

The slight shift of one eyebrow was his only acknowledgment that he'd heard her. He slipped on a pair of safety goggles and bent from the waist. With a tug on the recoil, he brought the chain saw roaring to life. The revving blasts indoors were deafening, and Christine wished she were wearing earplugs.

She took a step back as Bear lifted the chain

saw with an ease obviously gained through long practice. He pressed the saw against the snag, and an instant later the wood gave way, sending a shower of sawdust and splinters into the air.

Glancing at Christine who was standing still in the doorway, he shut off the motor, then lay the chain saw out of his way. "You can put your hands down now."

She dropped her hands to her sides abruptly. When his amused eyes met hers, a sting of embarrassment brushed her cheeks. "I'm not psychic," she stammered. "How am I supposed to know what to do?"

"Well"—his eyes ran over her lazily—"I assumed the upwardly mobile executive would not appreciate too many directives from—let's see if I have this right—an overgrown throwback to the sixties?"

Christine's lips parted as she recognized Percy's words. "You were eavesdropping?"

"If you haven't noticed, most of our windows are missing." He nodded to the gaping holes in the walls. "Besides, the little twerp's voice carries when he gets all riled up."

"I don't believe this." Christine released a huff of impatience.

Bear brushed at the sawdust clinging to his arms. "Well, if it's orders you want, you can get back to picking up around here."

"Oh, by all means." Christine grabbed up the cardboard box again. "If that's all you think I'm good for . . . picking up after you."

He scooped up a pair of work gloves and reached out to offer them to her. "Better wear these, or you'll ruin that twenty-dollar manicure."

"No thanks." Wood scraps thudded hollowly as she sailed them into the box.

He pressed the gloves into one of her hands. "Better listen to me, you'll be sorry if you don't wear some protection."

She paused for an instant to glance at the gloves. "I can't wear those. They're a dozen sizes too big." She handed them back to him as civilly as she could. "And I can do lots more around here than pick up trash. I am not helpless, if you haven't noticed."

"You have other skills?"

She tossed him a sidelong glance as she stopped to grab a chunk of drywall. "Never underestimate us yuppies. We're an ambitious, determined lot. Why, we pick up all manner of expertise as we crush each other in our mad race to the top of the heap."

She could have sworn she saw him grin before he turned his back to her. "So I've heard."

"So did I," she said with enough irony for him to know she'd overheard his disgruntled mutterings about her among other things.

Clearing his throat, he gazed at the cracked ceiling. "Perhaps I have been a bit hasty in my initial assessment." He took a firm stance, folded his arms across his prominent chest, and turned back to look at her. "Why don't you fill me in on your areas of . . . expertise."

As her initial irritation began to fade, she found herself wishing that she'd kept her mouth shut. She was usually not one to seek a confrontation. But it was too late to back down now. "When I was working on the other house—"

"What house was that?" he interrupted.

"Not far—a few miles south of Soquel."

He nodded. "Go on."

"As I was saying, I learned to remove wallpaper, hang wallpaper, paint." She noted that he wasn't looking impressed. "I repaired plaster, cleaned gutters." His expression remained unchanged. "I replaced ceiling tiles, put up insulation and dry-wall." At that, his brows lifted.

After a moment, he nodded. "Got any friends who can help out?"

"I'm working on that. Sarah had planned to ride over with me, but one of her clients got arrested again, and she had to tend to that."

"Arrested?"

"Sarah's a public defender. And she's a good worker. In fact, there are lots of people who want to donate their time and effort to this project."

Bear glanced at the emptiness around them. "Right. Standing room only."

"That will change, I can assure you." She was undaunted by the look of pure skepticism on his face. "Well, now that you know what I can do, are you going to assign me to something more produc-tive than gathering trash?"

"I might."

"You might?" The nerve of this man, she thought, for the tenth time. "It might interest you to know that you are the foreman on this job, not my drill instructor."

He looked as though he'd been about to say something else and suddenly changed his mind. "You have a problem taking orders?"

"I don't believe this." She stared at him. He was the rudest man she had ever met.

"Work crews usually get their orders from the foreman. I would have thought you'd be accus-tomed to a chain of command. Don't they have one at . . . ElectroFirst? That is where you said you worked, isn't it?"

She took a deep, steadying breath. "That is where I work," she said in measured tones. "And I'm quite familiar with the chain of command. However, there is a way to give an order so that it *feels* like a suggestion. People work better under such conditions." Her eyes hardened. "Employees retain a measure of dignity that way."

"Right."

His answers made her wonder if he'd understood a word she'd said.

"Well," he continued, "as I was saying, before I was *interrupted*, I might have you try something else *once* you get some work gloves that fit you."

Interrupted him! Well, maybe she had interrupted him in midsentence, but that was only because he wouldn't let her get a word in edgewise.

She glanced at her watch to signal she'd had enough. "Look, I'm hungry. I saw a convenience store on the way over. I'm going to run down and get some juice and raisins. You want anything?"

"Is it noon already?"

She shook her head. "Eleven-fifteen."

"We don't take a lunch break until noon."

"I'm not having lunch."

"Oh?" That look returned to his face.

"I eat six times a day."

"*Six* times a day?"

"Yes, *six* times a day."

"How come you're not fat?"

She sighed. He was impossible. "It's healthier if you don't bulk your system down with three square meals a day. If you eat six little meals, it keeps your energy level humming evenly along."

"Good Lord, sounds to me like a waste of time. Why not eat three meals and have it over with?"

"Well, you don't eat much. You eat minimeals, like little snacks."

He shook his head. "I thought those health nuts are preaching to cut out the snacks."

"Never mind." He was hopeless. She picked up her handbag and then headed for the door.

"By the way, while you're out, pick up some gloves." When she didn't respond, he felt compelled to add, "Not those flimsy cotton garden gloves, but some sturdy leather *work* gloves."

She paused, her hand on the screen door. "I think I can select a pair of suitable gloves." She was halfway through the door when she remembered her manners. She stopped in her tracks. "You want anything?" She glanced around. Hers was the only vehicle in sight. It would be rude to drive off and not at least offer to bring him back anything.

"No, thanks."

She saw him turn and head back toward his work. Breathing a sigh of relief, she stepped outside and crossed the porch. What she needed was a breather, a few minutes away from *Bear* Malone so that she could compose herself.

Who was he to make her feel guilty for taking a simple break? Who was he to make her feel guilty for driving a BMW, for not bringing gloves, and for not packing along snacks so she didn't have to drive to the local convenience store to purchase them?

It wasn't her fault that things weren't going according to plan. And planning was something she knew something about. She arranged her workdays and her weekends around a schedule that worked perfectly.

Yet, for some reason, she could not shake the disconcerting feeling that Bear Malone was going to mess up her agenda.

Two

At noon, Christine left once again for lunch at a small, neighborhood restaurant. She chose a table near a wall of windows, away from the groups clustered around the salad bar and the order counter.

She'd asked Bear if he'd like a ride and he'd said no, but his look told her that her six meals a day was getting on his nerves. Well, that was all right with her. Almost anything she did got on his nerves.

Sipping her herbal iced tea, she savored the relaxation that enveloped her. She was sprinkling nonfat salad dressing over her mixed green salad when a movement through the door caught her eye. Her hand froze in midair, her fingers tensed, and dressing spurted from the foil packet. She glanced down to find French dressing splattered across the front of her white T-shirt.

Bear Malone waved at her from the doorway, and she waved back with the foil packet still clenched in her palm. While he stood at the order counter with his back to her, she quickly grabbed a handful of paper napkins and sopped up the globs of dressing on her T-shirt.

For nonfat dressing, it was leaving behind dark, oily-looking smears. She hurriedly dipped her last napkin into her water glass. Surely the stains would come out if she wet them a bit. She dabbed at the splotches, leaving huge wet spots in her haste.

To her relief, most of the red dressing was disappearing. To her horror, the water was turning her white T-shirt into a transparent window, putting her lacy wisp of a bra on display.

Bear turned around from the counter, carrying his food tray in his hands. His eyes scanned the room as did hers. Every table and booth in the place was filled with hungry occupants from a tour bus parked outside.

She mentally groaned as he strolled in her direction.

He stopped when he reached her table. "No other seats available. Mind if I park here?" he asked.

She shrugged. "No, be my guest."

His gaze, distracted by the slight movement of her shoulders, shifted downward from her face, and his eyes widened as they fastened on the fullness of her breasts, barely concealed by two scallops of white lace.

"Don't mind if I do," he said as he lowered himself into the chair across from her. While his fingers worked open the foil wrapping surrounding his double cheeseburger, it was obvious he fought to keep his glance from returning to her.

"I . . . uh," she began, pulling her T-shirt away

from her skin. "I had a problem with the salad dressing."

Bear reached over and handed her the paper napkin from his tray. "Would you like more?" he asked pleasantly.

"Please . . ." She had never felt so foolish.

He rose and walked to the condiment counter and grabbed a handful of napkins. He handed them to her as he took his seat across from her.

"Thanks," she whispered.

His expression remained passive though he must have noted that while he'd been away from the table she'd tucked the napkin he'd given her into her neckline and spread it like a bib across her front.

"If you'll excuse me," she said as she rose from her chair. Holding the napkin in place with her fingertips, she headed for the ladies' room.

When she returned minutes later, she was wearing the same T-shirt, only now it was bone dry.

Bear didn't ask how she'd managed it, but after a few silent moments, she said, "Hand dryers."

The corners of his mouth lifted in a slight smile. She could see that she was too fancy for his taste, but apparently he could tolerate a woman who could laugh at herself.

For an instant, they glanced at each other's meals: Hers, a salad, heavy on the alfalfa sprouts and shredded carrots; his, a double cheeseburger deluxe, a large order of French fries, and a strawberry shake.

He poured a puddle of ketchup, dipped a large fry, and offered it to her.

"No, thanks."

"You sure? Those sprouts don't look like they'll hold you until your next meal."

They ate in silence for a moment, and he noticed she was still staring at his meal. "Something bothering you?"

"I was trying to guess the fat grams on your tray. There's enough there to carry me into next week." She heard the censure in her own voice and caught herself. She wasn't a health freak, she just adhered to sensible eating. "Excuse me, that was rude. What you choose to eat is entirely your business."

"Well, it's not seafood with Percy."

She shrugged.

"Known him long?" he asked casually.

"A few months. We came to California about the same time."

"From the same place?"

"No." She chuckled at the huge differences in their backgrounds. "I'm from Des Moines. Percy's from Boston. We were hired as management trainees at the same time."

"So," he said, selecting a couple of fries, "you're a trainee."

"Well, no. I'm a materials manager."

His glance lifted with interest. "What do you do?"

"I schedule component arrivals for assembly so that we can operate with a minimum of storage."

"Sounds hairy."

"It is at times." She thought about her job and added, "Well, most of the time."

"Hmmm," he murmured. "Six months on the job, and already a promotion."

He promotion was not something she would have brought up, but it had been the highlight of the past six months. She'd worked long hours, and the reward was sweet.

"And Percy," Bear said casually, adding ketchup to his hamburger, "has he been promoted too?"

"Not yet." In her opinion, Percy spent too little time working and too much time politicking his boss, but she wasn't going to say that. "In time, his contribution will be recognized."

Bear took a long pull on his shake and studied her over the rim of his cup. When he set the cup aside, it was as if he'd made a decision. "You know," he began, "the little twerp underestimates you."

Her gaze met the steady, appraising look in his eyes. If Bear Malone knew that he was overstepping his bounds, his expression didn't show it. "I know that Percy underestimates me," she replied, matching conjecture with candor.

"He underestimates you, and you don't mind." It was a statement, not a question.

She took another sip of tea. "No, that only makes it easy to stay one step ahead of him." She didn't add that it was even easier to stay a dozen steps ahead of Percy's amorous advances.

"So you can stay ahead of him." His tone seemed disinterested, almost clinical. "Does that work in the long run?"

"For the short term."

"Do you always choose companions for the short term?"

"Are you always so blunt?"

His brows lifted as if he were thinking about her question, then a smile touched the corners of his mouth. "I suppose I am." Then he ignored her question and his reply, and continued their conversation as if it were an interview, "So, today's career woman isn't looking for romance."

"Not this one." Her answer came quickly.

"So romance is dead. What a pity."

From the detachment in his voice, she couldn't tell whether romance mattered to him one way or the other. "Romance is a myth, a pleasant one, perhaps, but a myth just the same."

"Surely, you jest." He looked surprised. "I thought all little girls believed in Prince Charming."

"Some do. Some don't. I happen to belong to the latter group."

"And I bet you're happier that way."

"Since I'm a realist, yes, I think I'm happier."

He studied his last French fry. "Really?" His tone seemed somewhat distracted.

"My mother is a hopeless romantic, who believes in fairy tales, but she's not living one."

"Miserable, huh?"

"Not miserable." She fell silent for a moment. "Unfulfilled . . . bored might be more accurate. She gave up her dreams to become my father's housekeeper, maid, wife, whatever."

"She had you—a worthwhile trade-off for many women."

"Ha, a man's point of view. Really now, admit it: It's easy to like the status quo when everything is going your way. That's why my dad is so content . . . and exactly why my mother is so stifled."

"I assume your mother has confided how unhappy she is."

Christine put down her fork. "She doesn't have to. It's obvious. Besides, she's too loyal to say anything bad about my dad."

He nodded understandingly. "But you're not."

She smiled. "As I said, I'm a realist."

Suddenly, she felt awkward and exposed. It wasn't like her to get carried away, to reveal herself too much. This stranger knew a vital part of her past; more than that, he had a clue to what made her tick, and she knew nothing about him at all.

"And your mother—is she happy and fulfilled?"

He paused a beat. "I think she was." His face sobered. "She died a year ago."

"I'm sorry. I didn't mean to open any wounds." She had intended to pry, but not to hurt.

"My mother had a good life. She was a free spirit, divorced when I was five. We moved more than once, but she always managed to support us with her oil paintings. When she died, I came here from Colorado Springs to settle her accounts and wound up staying on."

Christine decided to change the subject. "You know, it's still crowded in here. I think others could use our table."

As they headed for the door, a girl behind the counter sang out, "Don't forget your cup, Bear." She leaned forward, extending a huge, insulated plastic cup.

"Thanks, Cheryl." Bear slid a tip across the counter with one hand took the cup in the other.

They stepped outside into the California sunshine. There wasn't a cloud in the sky, and the crisp, tangy Pacific breeze ruffled her hair as Christine started toward her car. "Want a lift or—" she angled him a glance filled with challenge— "are you afraid to ride with me?"

"No, I'm feeling brave." Opening the passenger door, he eyed the interior of the BMW warily.

"How am I supposed to fit in this coffee can?"

"You'll have to squeeze in."

Bending, he grunted as he eased his tall frame onto the contoured seat.

"Here." She reached to the floor on his side. "Let's move the seat back."

"Ugh," he muttered when the top of his head bumped along the roof as his seat slid back as far as its tracks would permit.

"There's a lever on your side, down low." She pointed toward his door. "If you press it and lean back, your seat should recline enough to give you some headroom."

He fumbled for a moment, his fingers searching for a lever he couldn't possibly see. Just as she decided to get out and come around to help him, he found it. "Ah," he said, tilting back, "that's better."

"Sorry," she murmured, cranking open the sunroof. "Three eighteens aren't the roomiest."

"I always figured these status cars would at least be comfortable." He sounded more surprised than critical.

As she released the emergency brake wedged between their seats, the back of her hand inadvertently brushed his thigh. She felt a jolt of electricity but covered it with conversation. "This model is the baby of the line."

He sighed. "Well, I suppose you'll get successively bigger ones as you climb the corporate ladder."

The assumption rankled, but she remained silent. It wouldn't do any good to tell him that her car was six years old, that she'd bought it directly from its first owner, that it still looked brand-new because she faithfully polished and maintained it.

True, she'd fallen in love with the car at first sight, but she'd bought it because it had been affordable. It had cost her far less than many of the newer low-budget cars on the market. And she had to be thrifty, since she was still making hefty monthly payments on the student loans she'd taken out to go to college.

As she backed out of the parking space, she reminded herself that she and Bear didn't have to like each other. So why, she wondered, did she feel this longing for his understanding?

She flicked on her blinker and waited for a break in the traffic.

"Turn right," he ordered.

"Why? The house is back to the left."

"I need to stop at the hardware store."

With a flick of her wrist, she switched her blinker to the right. When she got her break, she pulled out onto the street abruptly. The large cup he'd placed on the floor overturned, and the contents seeped between the crack of the seat. He reached to right it, but a dark stain was already spreading in a big circle on the pearl-gray carpet.

"Oops," was his only comment.

Gritting her teeth, Christine reached across him to pop open the glove compartment. She grabbed a stack of paper towels and handed them to him. "If you don't mind," she began, glancing from the road to the floor, "tamp down on these towels with your feet." She choked back the urge to curse. She'd never spilled food or drink in her car, and she'd taken pride in the fact that the interior looked as spotless as if it were in a showroom.

She stopped at the light at the corner and bent to sop up the moisture. Bear began to lean forward at the same moment, and their heads collided.

Christine cried out when her forehead thudded against his temple. Leaning back in her seat, she massaged a spot above her right eyebrow.

"I can get it," Bear assured her, pressing the towels against the carpet. "Sorry," he mumbled as an afterthought. "Kind of a neat nut, aren't you?"

"A neat nut?" If that was his attempt at humor, it didn't work with her.

"Sorry, I only meant—"

"You don't have to explain. I know what you meant, Mr. Malone. First, you call me a yuppie. Next, you dig me about my status car. Then, even after I bend the rule and let you bring a drink into my car . . . and you spill it," she added as if his making a mess was inevitable, "that makes me a neat nut."

He dabbed at the dark stain regretfully. "Hey, I can fix this so you'll never know it happened."

She gritted her teeth until her jaw ached. "I know it can be cleaned, that isn't the point."

He glanced out the window at the passing scenery. He was probably wishing he'd never accepted a lift.

As they approached the next corner he suddenly ordered her to turn. "Pull in there." He pointed to a small shopping center. "There's a space, right in front of the hardware store. There, on the left."

Wheeling the car into the shopping center, Christine winced as she heard brakes screeching around her.

She'd hardly switched off the motor before Bear was climbing out of the car. She sat in the car for a moment, watching him stride across the sidewalk. Halfway through the double doors of the hardware store, he glanced over his shoulder and casually motioned her to follow.

"Yes, master," she muttered, pulling the key

from the ignition. Reluctantly, she walked into the hardware store.

Bear glanced up from the end of the first aisle as she entered the store. "Over here."

She moved in his direction with deliberate slowness. "I'm coming master, I'm coming," she murmured in a wry undertone.

"Christine." He spoke as if he were speaking to a recalcitrant child. "Try these on." He handed her a pair of leather work gloves.

"I don't—"

"Just try them on," he interrupted smoothly. Then he turned and took a few steps down the aisle, scanning the shelves.

Sighing in resignation, Christine slipped her hands into the gloves, and flexed her long fingers. To her surprise, the gloves fit amazingly well. She was just removing them when a clerk approached.

"May I help you—"

Christine was about to answer when the clerk passed her by without a glance to stand next to Bear. ". . . Mr. Malone?"

"Yeah, how's it going, Shirley? We'll take the gloves the lady just tried on."

"May I take them to the register for you?" the young woman asked pleasantly, her eyes on Bear as she reached for the gloves in Christine's hand.

"Thanks." Bear summoned a warm smile for her. "We'll be along in a minute."

"I'll be waiting, Mr. Malone," she chirped, plucking the gloves from Christine and breezing to the front of the store.

Christine crossed her arms, and curiosity entered her eyes. "Everyone seems to know you."

Bear stopped to weigh out and bag a few pounds

of nails. "I've been in the area a few weeks working on the house." He shrugged.

"By yourself?"

"Most of the time."

"Well, that'll have to change." Her flair for organization had the wheels in her mind turning. "Progress is too slow working by yourself. What we need here is a team approach."

"No kidding." He shook his head and strolled away.

"There's going to be a project meeting next Thursday evening at seven," she said, following him. "The mayor has asked me to attend. Will you be there?"

He nodded and kept moving.

"We need to bring up a few things."

"Right," he mumbled, his interest in the conversation obviously taking a backseat to the array of items surrounding him. At the end of the aisle, he scanned the shelf, then looked over his shoulder at her. "Come here." His voice lacked the cheery note he'd used when speaking to the young clerk. Back again was the no-nonsense tone.

"You must be talking to me," she replied, taking a few steps toward him.

Placing a sack of nails on the floor, he reached for her hand.

"Wait a minute—what do you think you're doing?" She tried to pull her hand away, but his grip was firm as he turned her hand in his, running his thumb across her fingers and palm.

He looked into her puzzled eyes. "Well, you've messed them up good."

She glanced at her hand. "What do you mean?"

"You should've been wearing gloves this morn-

ing. Now your hands are nicked and they're going
to be sore as hell."

She withdrew her hand. "I think that's my
business."

"No, ma'am, it's my business too."

"How do you figure that?"

"At the moment you're the only volunteer I have.
You're no good to me if you're out of commission.
If you heal quickly and wear gloves, you *might* be
of some help." He pulled a tin from the shelf and
handed it to her. "You'll need to apply this liber-
ally several times today."

Her brows rose as she read the label, unable to
believe her eyes. "What is . . . udder ointment?"
Her jaw dropped as she stared at him. "Surely
you're not suggesting I . . ."

His face remained nearly expressionless as he
gazed down at her. "It is very healing."

"What makes you think I need *this*?" She held
up the tin. The picture on the label showed a
smiling Holstein cow that looked in imminent
need of milking.

Bear blinked and for an instant seemed on the
verge of blushing as he glanced down at the front
of her white T-shirt that less than an hour ago had
been transparent. "Oh, uh . . . you thought I
meant for you to . . . no, no . . . that's for your
hands."

"My hands?"

"Read the directions. That salve heals hands . . .
along with other things. I use it a lot."

"You do?" she asked incredulously.

"On my hands." He glanced around. She, too,
hoped no one was overhearing their conversation.
When she glanced down at the back of the tin,
Bear seized his opportunity to escape and headed

past her toward the front of the store. "I'll be at the register."

After a little careful reading, Christine discovered that the ointment was recommended for the hands of dairymen and others who worked with their hands.

Strolling to the cash register, Christine stood next to Bear while the clerk began ringing up the purchases. When Shirley reached for the gloves, Christine spoke up.

"Please ring those up separately along with this." Christine handed her the tin of ointment.

"Just ring it up together," Bear ordered.

"I don't want to use the project funding for personal items, so I'll pay for my things separately."

"The project funding?" Shirley asked, looking at Bear in confusion.

He shook his head. "Charge the nails as usual," he said quietly.

"Okay, Mr. Malone." She entered the amount, and Bear signed for it.

As Christine watched, Shirley rang up the gloves and ointment separately and Christine paid her.

Back in the car, she applied the sticky ointment to her reddened hands. "You want to drive?" She glanced at Bear. "I hate to get this goo all over the steering wheel."

"No thanks. Just slip on the gloves first."

"Okay."

He looked relieved. And she realized for the first time that day, she had taken his advice without question or comment.

Back at the house, they worked together applying strips of fiberglass to a badly cracked ceiling.

Bear nodded in satisfaction at the strips that

crisscrossed the ceiling like a spider web. "Tomorrow I'll give it a thin coat of plaster, and Monday it'll be ready for paint. You won't believe how good it will look, as smooth as a baby's—" He caught himself, glancing at her. "But then I guess you won't see the finished ceiling, will you?"

She met his look evenly. "I'll see it." She recognized the doubt in his face, and she heard it in his voice. She'd stuck it out all day, and he figured the novelty had surely worn off for her by now. He expected her to go back to her corporate world and joke with her friends at lunch about the Saturday she spent roughing it.

She glanced at the pink sky through the broken window. "It's getting dark." She slung her bag over her shoulder. "I better be on my way. Can I give you a lift?"

"You'd let me in your car after I spilled my coffee?" The corners of his mouth twitched as he arched a brow.

She shrugged. "I'm a risk taker. Besides, I happen to know that your thermos and your big cup are both empty."

He grinned. "You *are* a neat nut." As she started to protest, he lifted a hand. "But you didn't hear it from me."

She chuckled. "And you are hopeless."

"Then go on, get out of here. You've probably got a hot date, and I have a few things to do here before I head out."

She nodded and turned for the door. He hadn't said good-bye, but she could sense that he really didn't expect to see her again.

She sat in her car while the engine warmed up. Through the window, she saw the overhead light come on and then him walking across the room. A moment later, the sound of hammering split the air. As he nailed up a strip of ceiling trim, she watched him swing the hammer in a mesmerizing rhythm. Even from that distance, she thought she could see the muscles in his shoulders flex and stretch with each movement.

"Oh, brother," she murmured to herself, shifting into reverse, "I must be tired. Why else would I be sitting here gawking at a man like some moony-eyed teenager?

She backed out on the street. When she was nearly past the house, she stole one more glance over her shoulder at the man standing under a patch of light, working alone.

As she drove through the twilight she couldn't help wondering when he would be finishing up. He wasn't being compensated for his labor, but he was putting in long hours just the same. The men where she worked sometimes worked long hours, but never without pay.

Percy had been right about one thing. Bear Malone was different.

Three

The following Thursday evening Christine Brighton swung her car into the first parking space she could find downtown. As she locked the doors, she checked her watch again, regretting that she hadn't had time to run by the apartment to change clothes. If she hurried, she could still make her seven o'clock meeting in the mayor's conference room. Her high heels clicked across the sidewalk as she strode into the lengthening evening shadows.

Smoothing her suit jacket, she reached into her pocket for her roll of antacids. Today she'd skipped lunch and had to survive on vending-machine snacks. Tension was climbing up her neck and settling into a throb at the back of her head.

The phone on her desk had rung all afternoon. After the seventh fax, she'd prayed—to no avail—for the machine to break down. A typhoon had delayed a crucial shipment from the Orient, and she'd had to deal with a production staff that needed those components for the completion of their current project. Two truckloads of goods from the Midwest had arrived a day early, and she'd had to supervise the unloading herself.

If she'd had enough time to take a break, she might have called the mayor to excuse herself from the meeting. But she didn't want to cancel. Broken promises were the reason so many volunteer projects failed. When things got hectic, they were the easiest thing to call off. And she'd promised herself from the beginning that she wouldn't do that.

For as long as she could remember, she'd wanted to get behind a cause and see it through, a project that would make the world a better place. She'd worked part-time during her college years, so she'd had little time for civic contributions.

But when she'd graduated, she'd promised herself that she would *do something.* She'd considered the Peace Corps, but she felt obligated to repay her college loans as soon as possible. The idea of fund-raising for some anonymous charity had held little appeal for her. She preferred hands-on control; she wanted to actually see the results.

Down deep, she feared that if she did not get involved now, the dream would die. Renovating run-down buildings, converting them into safe, pleasant, affordable housing was the venture she'd been looking for, and she'd volunteered at the grass roots stage. She wasn't about to drop out now.

She knocked on the open door to the conference room and walked in. Mayor Casteel rose from the round table to meet her halfway across the room. "Christine." He shook her hand and smiled warmly as he turned to introduce her to the three council members who politely rose to greet her.

Mayor Casteel, a silver-haired man in his fifties, held a chair for her beside his. She smoothed her slim skirt as she sat down. "I hope I haven't kept you gentlemen waiting."

"No, no," Mayor Casteel said in his soft-spoken way. "We were just about to begin. But first we want you to know how much we appreciate your interest in our new project. We need young people like you to get behind these kinds of projects and make things happen."

She nodded. "I'm looking forward to contributing my share of the work."

"We feel fortunate to have you. I know that with your enthusiasm and gift for organization we can count on you to recruit others."

"I've already started a calling list."

"Very commendable." The mayor nodded at the council member next to him. "Don't you think so, Dave?"

"Why, yes. I understand from some of my business associates that you've solicited the donation of supplies from various lumberyards and stores in the area."

Christine smiled. "I've discovered that businesses sometimes receive goods that because of some slight defect cannot be sold to the public. Many times they're willing to donate them to take a charitable deduction." She'd already hit up her own company several times.

The councilman passed his business card across the mahogany table. "I think our company could help out. Ask for me when you call."

"Thank you. I'll do that."

There was a thud across the room, and Christine glanced up, startled. Bear Malone appeared in the doorway. In his haste, his heavy work boot had grazed the door frame. As usual, he seemed larger than life, especially when the mayor, a foot shorter, stood to greet him.

Bear politely shook hands all around, but his eyes kept returning to Christine. His eyes seemed to miss nothing, especially the fact that when she was sitting down her straight skirt rode up her thighs.

She crossed her legs as an excuse to tug at her hem. When she glanced up again, she found him still looking at her. He glanced at her hemline and nodded what she took to be his approval.

To her dismay, she could feel a flush of warmth creeping up her neck. She glanced out the window, hoping that he wouldn't notice her blushing. It annoyed her that she couldn't control her reaction to him. *I've had a hard day,* she reminded herself, *so naturally my nerves are on edge. That's the only reason his staring is getting to me.*

She took a deep breath to compose herself. Though she willed herself not to, she glanced casually his way again. He was watching her over the heads of the councilmen between them, and when their eyes met, the corners of his mouth lifted with what looked like amusement to her.

She scowled, and he had the audacity to grin at her, that lopsided grin that came to him so easily, that foolish smile that probably thrilled all the beach bunnies. Well, not her, she vowed, glancing away.

Christine pulled her hand out of her pocket and stared at the empty wrapper of antacids. It occurred to her that she might have another roll in her handbag. She was leaning way over to reach for her purse under her chair when she heard the mayor's voice nearby.

"I assume you've already met Mr. Malone?"

"What?" She raised up as abruptly as if she'd been caught shoplifting. Her glance moved to Bear. "Oh. I . . . of course, we've met."

The men were standing in a semicircle around her chair. She glanced from face to face expectantly. There was an awkward pause while she wondered what else she'd missed while she'd been digging into her purse. She looked down at the empty wrapper she still clutched in one hand. Self-consciously, she shoved it back into her pocket. A flush of embarrassment followed as she wondered why she'd done that.

Why did everything seem to go wrong when Bear Malone entered a room? How could he, without even saying a word to her, make her feel so awkward and foolish? *I need some sleep, an uninterrupted twenty-four hours. That's all that's wrong with me.*

The men began to take their seats around the table. Bear followed the mayor's gesture and took a seat beside Christine. She registered a small measure of satisfaction when she saw him pass his hand over the top of his head and down his arms to brush the wood flecks and plaster dust from his hair and shirt before he sat down. Obviously, he'd come to the meeting straight from work and hadn't had time to change. It pleased her that perhaps he wasn't feeling one-hundred-percent confident about himself either.

"Let's get right down to business, shall we?" Mayor Casteel began. When he received agreeable nods from around the table, he continued. "First of all, we consider ourselves lucky to have you, Mr. Malone. If it weren't for you, we wouldn't have our one-home renewal successfully completed. A wonderful young family is moving in this weekend, and they are thrilled. This is their first home. Up until now, they've lived in a government-subsidized apartment, not an ideal environment for raising children. They asked me to tell you that they love all the extras that you built into their home. They'd like for you to stop by." The mayor turned apologetic. "I hope it's all right that I gave them your name."

Bear nodded. "I'm glad they're pleased."

Christine had driven by the house but had never been inside, but she'd seen the pictures taken before and after.

The mayor looked pointedly at Bear. "I want to assure you, Mr. Malone, that we are going to see to it that you aren't working alone. You practically reconstructed that first house all by yourself, and we don't want you getting burned out on us, do we?" His gaze swept over the councilmen.

"Certainly not," one replied.

"No, we wouldn't want that," agreed the man sitting on Christine's left side.

A third nodded vigorously.

"Of course," the mayor continued, "we want you to be in full control of the project from beginning to end. You are the boss, the foreman, whatever you want to call yourself."

Bear shrugged. "Titles don't mean much to me."

The mayor nodded. "Well, I think I can speak for all of us when I say that as soon as the project receives a cash donation, and it will now that it's getting some publicity, we'll want to give you a salary. It won't be what you deserve, I'm sure, but we want you to have it just the same."

Bear shook his head. "If you get some cash,

spend it on building supplies. I'm doing okay financially."

The mayor cleared his throat, looking a bit unsure as to how to proceed. It was obvious that he felt it inappropriate to inquire about a man's finances. "I see," he added. "That's certainly generous of you."

Bear settled back in his chair in a way that indicated that he didn't intend to elaborate.

"Well, Mr. Malone, your dedication and skill are certainly the reasons that we've put you in charge." The mayor turned his attention to Christine. "And you, young lady, will play an equal part in the management of this project."

"Anything I can do to help."

"Frankly, Miss Brighton, you can be a great deal of help. I'm aware of your dedication to this project, and we can use your skill in recruiting and soliciting."

Christine caught Bear's grin in her direction. She looked up to see the wry lift of his brow. Why did the mayor have to mention recruiting? Showing up at the house all by herself was certainly no proof of her skill in that area. Still, she was not going to let her disappointing start—or Bear—faze her. She lifted her chin a fraction higher and looked back at the mayor who was opening the manila folder before him.

"Now," the mayor said, consulting his notes, "this is the way I see it." Christine found herself straining her eyes to glimpse at his penciled notes. "The two of you should cochair this project together from beginning to end."

Christine's head snapped up at the same moment that Bear did a double take.

"What?" she said.

The mayor looked up with a mild expression. "We think it makes perfect sense."

Christine glanced around to see the three councilmen nodding in unison.

The mayor smiled at her before his gaze included Bear. "You are both fully dedicated to this project. Both of you have skills that we must have to make it a success. I think you should share the authority equally, don't you?"

Christine looked at Bear. His expression was grim, his brows drawn together. For some reason, the fact that he seemed none too pleased made her feel better. Of course, he'd want all the control. So far, she'd seemed little more than a step-and-fetch-it helper to him, hardly worth minimum wage if she were being paid. It probably irked him to see her get equal billing. She was about to insist that he be given full authority until she'd seen that scowl on his face.

She turned to the mayor and smiled. "Thank you, Mayor Casteel. I'm sure that you and the councilmen will not regret your decision. I'm sure that Mr. Malone is as eager as I to share the burden of this project?" She left the lilt of a question at the end, in hopes of forcing him to respond verbally.

His gaze met hers levelly. Suddenly, his brows lifted and his scowl disappeared. His smile was as smooth as his voice. "It would be my pleasure to work with Miss Brighton."

Christine found herself wondering if she should have laid it on so thick.

There was a brief pause before Bear continued. "After the countless hours Ms. Brighton has put in on this project, it is only fitting that she have a major share of the responsibilities."

Her head whipped around, and the look she sent him was indignant. They both knew that she'd spent exactly one day on the project. His tone and expression appeared mild enough for the mayor and the councilmen, but she recognized the weight of sarcasm in his words.

Obviously, he thought she had lobbied the mayor for a lion's share of the credit for the project. For some reason known only to him, he was sharing it with her while letting her know that he knew she didn't deserve it. Any fool could see that he didn't want or appreciate her help. If he had said that up front, she would have respected it and quietly done her share in the background, the way she would have preferred anyway. But she'd be darned if she would let him slam her like this and get away with it.

She turned to the mayor and smiled warmly. "Well, it seems that Mr. Malone and I are in perfect agreement, as usual." Her glance touched Bear briefly before returning to the others. "We were fortunate to hit it off from the beginning. Why, the way Mr. Malone went out of his way to make me feel welcome, the way we worked together like a well-oiled machine," she shrugged, "you would have thought we were soul mates."

Bear nodded amiably, and his voice held only a trace of irony. "It was amazing all right."

"Gentlemen," the mayor addressed the councilmen, "I take this as a good omen." After they all nodded agreeably, the mayor closed his folder. "I'm happy to say that this concludes the business of our meeting."

• • •

At nine o'clock the following Saturday, Christine arrived at the house, dressed in faded jeans and a sweatshirt. She entered without knocking. Her footsteps echoed in the empty rooms as she moved through them looking for him. "Hunting for Bear," she mumbled under her breath. She'd dreaded this confrontation all week.

She saw a light burning in a small bedroom upstairs and headed in that direction. Anything she might have been prepared to say died on her lips as she paused in the doorway.

Bear was down on one knee, bent over a baby cradle. She silently watched him methodically massage a rag over each spindle down one side.

There was no sign that he was aware of her presence until he spoke. "Well, Ms. Brighton, ready to work?"

She crossed her arms and leaned against the door. "Yes."

He gave her a quick glance and continued polishing the cradle.

"What are you doing?" she asked.

"Giving it a hand-rubbed oil finish. Found this in the attic and replaced the broken spindles. Figured it'll come in handy for some family."

"Where should I start?" she asked.

"Did you bring anyone with you?"

"Volunteers?" She shook her head. "I have a crew lined up for next weekend. It seems everybody needed a few days to arrange schedules."

He nodded. "You can start by picking up downstairs."

Of course, she thought, *I can pick up the downstairs.* "Have supplies arrived this week?"

"No supplies and no helpers."

She turned on her heel and headed for the stairs. There was nothing she could say to that.

She gathered up chunks of debris, including his discarded soda cans, and sorted out the trash before discarding it into bins. Since her main task was to clean up, she figured the least she could do was sort it for recycling when possible.

She heard a large truck pull up outside, and she walked out onto the porch. A big smile lit her face when she recognized that this was the contribution that Barston Lumber Co. had promised her.

She helped the driver carry in the surplus that the owner had agreed to give to the project: Four slightly dented doors, several boxes of assorted nails, a crate of ceiling tiles, a dozen cans of misordered paint, an armload of wallpaper rolls from a discontinued line, and three boxes of items that for one reason or another had been returned.

She tried to tip the driver, but he waved her money away. "No, ma'am, it's the least I can do. Hope you can use the supplies."

"Indeed we can. Tell your boss thanks again."

No sooner was the truck pulling out of the driveway before Bear appeared in the doorway. "What's going on?"

She shrugged. "Barston sent us some surplus."

Soon Bear was lifting lids and unpacking boxes and she was helping him organize the materials. She dusted her hands off on her jeans. "Well, what do you think? Can we use some of this stuff?"

"Looks real promising." His blue eyes sparkled like a kid's on Christmas morning as he held a tile up to the cracked ceiling. "This will look nice, and it'll cover a multitude of sins at the same time." He placed the tile back in the box and glanced up at her. "You arranged this?"

"It was Mr. Barston's idea," she replied evenly.

"But you planted the idea."

She shrugged, and he cocked his head in a way that indicated his approval. "Any day you get somebody to send us supplies like this, I'm grateful."

Her brows lifted in mock surprise. "Grateful enough . . . to extend a favor?"

He crossed his arms and looked at her. "That depends on the favor."

"The deal is . . . you let me do something useful around here, besides pick up trash."

He grinned. "Like what?"

"Like whatever you're working on, you teach me to do. That way I can be of some real help, at least until the reinforcements arrive."

"The reinforcements," he repeated. "Are there really going to be any reinforcements?"

She realized that actions, not words, were what counted with this man. "This week supplies." She gestured around her, knowing better than to make promises. "Next week, who knows? You just have to have a little faith, Malone."

"Okay, Miss Brighton." He turned around. "If you want work, you got it."

She smiled in satisfaction. Things were looking up. First, the supplies had been delivered, and now she'd be included in the actual renovation.

She stayed close on his heels to discourage him from changing his mind as he led the way into the small bathroom. When he reached the back wall, he picked up what looked like giant tongs and faced her.

"Now what?" she asked, hoping that the glint in his eye was not homicidal.

"Now," he said, "we kneel."

She glanced down at the old rusty toilet that stood between them.

"You're kidding, of course."

He shook his head gravely and knelt on one side of the old commode. He pointed to the floor on the other side of the bowl.

She hesitated, then went to her knees. "What are we doing here?"

He looked into her eyes, and his lips twitched with what she figured was concealed amusement. "Your mission," he began in a serious tone, "since you've decided to accept it, is to help me remove the broken toilet seat so we can replace it with a new one."

"Oh." It wasn't exactly what she'd had in mind, but she'd gotten herself into this mess, and she was not going to give him the satisfaction of her complaining about it.

"I've already removed the screw on my side, but the threads are worn on your side. I can twist and twist, but until I can get a grip on that bolt from underneath, I can't remove the screw. The problem is with that built-in cabinet so close, there isn't enough room for me on that side."

So he'd already tried it by himself and hadn't succeeded. The only reason he was involving her at all was because this particular task required two.

She'd swallowed her pride and asked to be included. Now she realized that he probably would have had to ask her for assistance sooner or later. She wished that she'd held out just a little longer. It would have been nice if he'd had to ask for her help. Better yet, it would be nice to hear him *beg* her to help him. "In my dreams," she muttered bitterly.

"What?"

"Nothing." She glanced around warily. The setting was unpleasant. Beneath her knees, the green linoleum was cracked and curling. The air was musty, and they were surrounded by shadows.

"Here." He passed her a pair of pliers. "Use these to get a grip on that rusty bolt." After positioning his screwdriver on the head of the screw at the back of the toilet seat, he looked at her expectantly.

"Where?"

He looked confused. "Where what?"

"Where's this bolt I'm supposed to get a grip on?"

He waited as if she were about to throw a punch line to a joke. When she didn't supply one, he cleared his throat. "The bolt is underneath." When her eyes failed to register understanding, he continued. "See the screw here that I'm about to twist?"

She nodded.

"The bolt is attached to the screw . . . below."

"How am I supposed to see it?"

"Well, you're small enough to wedge a shoulder in there and look underneath."

She drew back. "It's nasty under there."

He nodded slowly.

"You don't expect me to . . . what if there's a mouse or a spider or something?" She hated herself for sounding so typically female, but it was nasty under there.

He passed her a flashlight, without comment.

"That's all I need," she said brightly, squaring her shoulders as though she'd walk into hades itself if she had a flashlight. She flicked on the light and slowly eased her shoulder and head down for a look. If someone had told her she'd be so nervous about looking behind a toilet, she would have laughed. But that would have been five minutes ago.

"See it?"

Reluctantly, she slid a little lower. "Yeah, I see it." The bolt was wedged halfway up the long metal spiral.

"Do you think you could get hold of that bolt . . . oh, say sometime in the next hour or so?"

"There's no need for sarcasm." She wriggled to get the pliers into position. "Got it."

He began twisting with the screwdriver. After a moment, he exhaled sharply. "You're not holding on tight enough. The bolt is spinning. We're getting nowhere."

"Okay, okay, don't get all bent out of shape." She set the flashlight on the floor and gripped the pliers with both hands.

"Ready?" he asked.

"Ready," she blurted impatiently. "Just screw away." She immediately regretted her choice of words. To make matters worse, instead of politely ignoring her remark, he chuckled.

"An interesting thought."

To release her frustration, she put a death grip on the pliers and saw the long screw start backing out as he twisted it from above. A minute later, Bear removed the broken toilet seat.

"You can come up now," he said.

She wasn't sure she wanted to show her face, but she was eager to unbend from the pretzel shape she'd forced herself into. Sitting up, she refused to meet his glances. Instead she watched his hands unpack and position the new toilet seat.

He handed her a bolt. "Now, thread this onto the

screw till it feels tight. Then give it a half-twist with the pliers."

She bent over and did as he'd instructed, and he did the same on the other side. While their heads were bent close to the floor, her eyes met his once briefly. Quickly, she glanced away and raised up.

"That should do it," he said, brushing off his hands as he stood up.

She sat on her heels and stretched her back until the vertebrae popped back into place. When she started to rise, he held out his hand to help her up. She hesitated only an instant before taking it and letting him pull her to her feet.

Gathering his tools, he walked to the front door. She followed along, glancing automatically along the way for trash she'd need to gather.

His glance skimmed the broken screen in the front door. "I think we can salvage the door if we replace the screen."

She looked at the object in question. "I'd agree except the latch mechanism is stuck. It won't catch."

He paused, examining the latch. "It can be fixed." Opening the door, he ran his glance over the perimeter. "What's important is the frame, and it's sound. We can replace the screen."

She was surprised he'd used the word *we*. She wondered if he intended to include her from now on or keep her around for trash collection and toilet repairs. The screen door certainly had more appeal. She shrugged. "I don't suppose it would hurt to try."

"I suppose in your neighborhood, you simply dial for a handyman to replace the door. Not everyone can afford the luxury."

She shook her head. "Here we go again."

He had the door halfway off its hinges when he turned to face her. "Are you trying to tell me something?"

"No, I'm telling you. You're a snob."

"Me?" The look on his face was incredulous.

"Yes, you. You're so sure you've got me figured out. I'm the spoiled, indulgent yuppie, squandering the nation's wealth while children of the world are starving. Well, that's not fair. You don't know me at all. The way I see it, you're the snob, not me."

He hooked his hands on his hips, glaring. "And just how do you figure that?"

"Your mind is closed." The topic was open, and she was on a roll. "You don't see me as an individual. Instead you have me pigeonholed. You think you know who I am, what I like, and what I don't like. Admit it, Malone. You plain old don't like me."

"Lady, as far as I'm concerned, you can be whoever you want to be. The way I see it, we don't have much in common, plain and simple."

She crossed her arms. "So that justifies everything, doesn't it? This way you can continue to make all the wisecracks you want to about my lifestyle, as you see it, and act superior." She shook her head and turned on her heel.

"Hey, I'm not the one driving the expensive car, wearing the designer labels, going to the exclusive clubs."

She spun around. "No, you're the one knocking my freedom of expression. You're the judge and jury here. Not me."

His brows drew together. "I don't know where you get off calling me a snob."

She took a step forward. "I'll tell you where. You

judge my lifestyle without ever trying it. How can you know what I'm like? It's so easy to condemn without knowing. How in all fairness can you judge the worth of something if you haven't tried it?"

He exhaled in a huff, then folded his arms and scowled back at her. "You know, you may have a point." Her chin lifted a notch higher. "But before you get too smug, just ask yourself if what you're accusing me of could be said of you too."

Her eyes narrowed. "What are you getting at?"

"You don't know my world any better than I know yours."

She cocked her head to one side. "The point being?"

"I don't back down easy. You best not challenge me to do anything you're not sure you can handle yourself."

She stood her ground and looked him in the eye. "The arrogance of the male of the species never fails to amaze me." She wasn't about to back down either. "I wonder if you could live even one day of my life."

"I can take anything you can take."

"Prove it."

"All right, but remember, that can work both ways." They stood facing each other, arms crossed, feet apart. His head tilted down, her chin tilted up.

Somewhere in her head a little voice warned her to back off, but she tossed caution aside. "So, we put it to a test?"

"I'm listening."

"Okay. It seems our days are tied up with this project."

He nodded.

"Therefore, I propose we take an evening or two and see who's the real snob here."

"No problem. What do you suggest?"

She thought for a moment. "One evening I go somewhere of your choice, participate in some recreation or entertainment of your choosing. Another evening I designate where we go, what we do. Afterward, we'll just see who's flexible, who has an open mind." She looked at him pointedly. "And which of us has tunnel vision."

"Brighton, prepare to eat crow." He turned, reaching for his hammer. "You're on."

Four

"Well, that was pretty stupid, Christine," Christine muttered as she stood before her closet in her silk undies, trying to find something to wear.

You let your mouth take control of your brain, her conscience answered.

She hated to admit it, but it was true. She was usually cautious and logical. All that had changed in the past weeks. Maybe it was due to the heavy stress on her job lately. She shook her head, unwilling to give in to self-deception. No, to be honest, she'd have to admit that she'd begun to lose control of her emotions the day she'd met Bear Malone.

He was as responsible as she was for this childish challenge to unveil the true snob. She released a long sigh, feeling a fraction better having someone else to blame beside herself. it occurred to her that she might have more to blame on Bear Malone after this evening. It was becoming increasingly difficult for her to ignore the fact that he was a compellingly interesting man.

She shoved aside her premonitions of impending doom and reached into her closet. The man's arrogance alone would be enough to quell any attraction she might feel for him.

With a renewed sense of determination, she chose a pair of faded jeans and a cotton turtleneck. Wearing old, comfortable favorites would help her feel relaxed—a good idea, she decided, since everything else about this evening was making her feel uncomfortable.

She could still see the smug challenge in Bear's eyes when he'd suggested that she join him for a Friday night on the town, an evening filled with activities of his choosing. Though he hadn't said it—hadn't needed to—the sneer in his voice had effectively implied that she couldn't last through one evening before throwing up her hands and admitting that she was hopelessly biased against anything that wasn't exclusive, imported, or expensive.

She flipped to the yellow pages to double-check the address of the bowling alley he'd chosen. A sleazy alley on the sleazy side of town, naturally. As she headed to her car, she was glad that she'd suggested that she drive herself there to meet him. That way she could retain her independence and keep the evening from remotely resembling a date.

Bear Malone walked into the bowling alley fifteen minutes before Christine was to arrive. While he stood for a moment scanning the atmosphere, a ripple of guilt passed through him. He had chosen the oldest, seediest, smoke-filled bowling alley he could find. There were several bright, clean, modern facilities more conveniently located for both of them. However, he had picked this one to make a point. Someone like Christine Brighton would be disgusted by the run-down condition of this establishment, and its patrons would be a major turnoff to her.

He squared his shoulders and shrugged off his guilt. She was the pretentious one, not he. An evening here would make that obvious even to her.

For some reason, he was aware of the moment she walked into the place. His gaze moved across the room to her slender silhouette framed in the doorway where she paused to get her bearings. With a measure of irritation he could not even fathom, he noticed that he was the only man to notice her presence. He didn't understand it. She was good-looking, damn good-looking, so why did the other men fail to notice her? Bad taste, he decided. She was too classy for these guys.

Her eyes found him, and they exchanged a brief nod of recognition. As he approached her, he thought he could detect a glance of dismissal as her eyes roamed her surroundings.

It was just the reaction he had expected from a woman like her. When he reached her side, he paused an instant, then asked, "Care for a brew?"

"Love one, thanks." She walked with him to the nearby bar.

Bear looked at her expectantly. "Light or regular?" He was prepared to inform her that this bar had never stocked champagne wishes or caviar dreams.

She shrugged slightly. "Whatever you're having will be fine."

He nodded to the young man tending bar. "Two bottles—the usual."

"Your usual?" The bartender looked confused. "What's that, buddy?"

Bear was annoyed, but changed the order. "Two bottles of Warrior, buddy."

The bartender lifted two long-necked dark bottles out of the cooler and snapped off the caps. Bear laid cash on the bar and handed Christine a bottle. She turned the chilled bottle in her hand. "Warriors' Brew? I've never heard of it."

"I drink it all the time." He took a swig, wincing at the unfamiliar taste as he glanced at the assorted characters hanging around the bar.

Christine lifted the bottle to her mouth and cautiously took a sip. The mixture had a heavy flavor of hops and the crisp tingle of carbonation.

"Like it?" he asked casually.

"Sure." She thought she saw a wry twist at the corner of his mouth before he glanced down. "You'll need shoes."

Carrying her bottle, she followed him to a counter. Behind it was a rack holding hundreds of pairs of well-worn bowling shoes. A paunchy, middle-aged man glanced her up and down. "Size eight?"

"Seven and a half, narrow," Christine returned coolly.

He'd already turned and was taking down a pair from the shelf. He slid them across the counter without looking at her. "Seven and a half it is. If you want 'em narrow, tighten the laces."

"Thank you," she replied evenly, determined to see this asinine challenge through. She pulled her coin purse out of her pocket, but before she could get it open, Bear had slapped the money on the counter.

"I'll get it," she protested. "I'd prefer to pay my own way."

The man behind the counter lifted his heavy brows.

Scooping up the shoes, Bear handed them to her. "I'm paying."

"Thank you."

"You're welcome."

She stood for an instant, watching him walk away, annoyed by the high-handed way he managed everything. But then she reminded herself that just such an attitude was exactly what she should expect from him. With a sigh of resignation, she trailed behind him.

Perching on a bench beside Bear, she pulled off her tennis shoes, then took a deep breath before slipping her feet into the bowling shoes that at least a thousand people had worn before her. She tightened the laces snugly. Bear gestured toward the rows upon rows of bowling balls lining one wall. The rack contained all colors, sizes, and weights. "Pick your weapon, Brighton."

Drawing another deep breath, Christine stood up and followed him to the rack of balls. She couldn't help noticing how many women turned their heads to stare admiringly at Bear's imposing, broad-shouldered physique. Well, he was good-looking, she'd never tried to tell herself otherwise. Ignoring the envious glances coming her way, she concentrated on selecting a ball.

Bear lifted one ball from the rack, replaced it, and tried another, testing each for weight and balance. "This one feels pretty good," he said after a moment. "You found one yet?"

"So many choices." She sighed as she lifted one

and then another, trying out various configurations of finger holes and weights.

"Well, they keep the kiddie balls—the eight pounders behind the counter. Want one of those?"

"No thanks." She reached for a basic black model. "This one will do nicely."

Bear looked at her choice, then back to her. "You sure?"

Her eyes met his evenly. "Positive."

Shrugging, he walked back to the lane. "Want any instructions before we begin?"

She shook her head. "No thank you."

"Bowl often, do you?"

"Not often."

Her response caught him off guard. He would have bet his last dime she'd never been in a bowling alley in her life. "You serious? Have you bowled before?"

Her lips moved to form a hint of a smile. "You don't think I could possibly know anything about bowling, do you?" She shrugged. "I'm not good, if that's what you're worried about."

"Worried? Me? Ha." He sounded indignant, but his gaze swung away. "You've never been here before, have you?"

She was tempted to point out that she strongly suspected that he hadn't either. No one had greeted him in a familiar way, the bartender had had no idea what to serve him when he'd asked for "the usual," but she decided to keep quiet. He was just trying to make a point he wasn't going to make.

"You've read me all wrong. I have no problem with this place, Bear. In fact, I like it." She took a noisy sip out of her bottle. "Just as much as you do."

"You're up," he said gruffly.

She got to her feet, rubbing the palms of her hands on the back of her jeans. With a tingle of apprehension, she stepped up onto the slick wooden approach and lifted the bowling ball from its cradle. The thing weighed a ton. For a long moment, she stood feet together, the bowling ball poised atop the heels of her hands. Praying that she wouldn't make a total fool of herself, she focused on the pins at the end of the long, narrow lane.

She inhaled and released her breath slowly, hoping to clear her mind. It had been a long time. She hoped that she could remember the routine. *Just hit the headpin, Christine.*

"You taken root up there?" Bear groused.

With slow, firm steps, she moved forward, bending from the waist and swinging her right arm in a wide arc. She held on to the ball a fraction too long. When she released the ball, it bounced loudly down the smoothly polished planks. She clenched her hands into fists and drew them up under her chin, willing the ball to stay on course. "Please," she whispered, "not the gutter."

Moving in slow motion, the ball lost momentum and began wobbling and weaving, first right, then left, looking smaller and smaller while the pins loomed larger and larger. Ten feet from the pins, the ball made a sharp left and thudded into the gutter.

"Darn it," she muttered. With determined effort, she squared her shoulders and pasted on what she hoped was an agreeable expression. She spun around and returned to the bench. As she passed Bear, she smiled. "Your turn."

"You got another ball."

"I knew that." She smoothed her blouse over her

jeans, then walked back to the ball return. The second ball knocked the tenpin down. Nothing else.

"Good shot," Bear muttered as she returned to the bench.

"My arm isn't warmed up yet."

"Yeah, right."

Bear lifted his bowling ball as easily as if it were a tennis ball. She watched him move through his steps with agile grace, sending his ball on a straight course. Seconds later, his ball crashed into the pins, toppling all but one.

With his next roll, the ball moved down the lane as though it operated on remote control, neatly picking off the tenpin. She tried to look pleasant as he sat down and picked up his pencil to mark the score sheet.

"Not bad," she said, moving past him. As she reached down for her ball, two brawny forearms from someone in the adjacent lane came into her view. She glanced up sharply. Those forearms were attached to bulging biceps, each sporting somewhat risqué tattoos.

"You know, babe," the tattooed man said congenially, "if you'll just bend forward more and put a little more lift on the ball, it won't bounce on ya like that."

"Ooookay," she said. She paused for a moment, concentrating on the headpin. The man, though rugged in appearance, seemed merely to want to offer some helpful advice.

She had the sinking feeling that everyone in the building had stopped what they were doing to watch her. That's ridiculous, she told herself. She could hear the thunder of balls rolling down lanes, colliding with pins. She reassured herself that if everyone had stopped what they were doing, she would be surrounded by silence.

She moved slowly, keeping her gaze fixed on the red-and-white pins at the end of the lane. She tried to block out everything, but the fact that Bear Malone was watching her was impossible for her to discount completely.

She took the stranger's advice and tried to put more lift on the ball. Seconds after she released the ball, she felt encouraged when it didn't bounce. To her relief, it wasn't heading straight for the gutter either. Her eyes grew wide as the ball neared the pins. Holding her breath, she heard the ball smack and three pins toppled. She sighed gratefully. Unfortunately, the three pins she'd picked off were in the middle of the formation, leaving a horrendous split, one that would be nearly impossible for a pro to pick up. But anything was better than the agony of another gutter ball.

As she returned, the tattooed man gave her a thumbs-up. She smiled and looked at Bear, whose head was bent as he busily recorded her score. Four pins in two frames; she wasn't exactly blazing her way into the bowling Hall of Fame, she conceded.

As she reached for her ball again, she heard a sharp whistle and glanced up. The tattooed man sat slouched on a bench, one hand caressing the shoulder of the blonde sitting next to him, the fingers of his other hand wrapped around the long neck of a beer. With the bottle, he gestured toward the pins on the right, indicating that aiming for them would be Christine's best bet.

She nodded and picked up her ball, focusing on the cluster of pins on the right as she released the ball. To her amazement, she knocked down two of them before the ball tipped into the gutter.

As she sat down, Bear said, "Not bad."

She smiled, feeling much better. "Thanks. I think my arm's warm now."

Bear looked down to record her score then rose to take his turn. This time he missed four pins on his first roll. He looked a bit tense on his next roll. Something about his rhythm was off, and he left three pins standing.

He shrugged as he returned to his seat. Quietly, she stood and walked to her ball. As she bent to pick it up, the tattooed man appeared beside her. "Hey, babe, looks like I got you throwin' bullets while the ol' man's game is startin' to slip."

The corners of her mouth lifted slightly. "Your advice helped."

"Keep it up." He gave her another thumbs-up, then turned to join his girlfriend who had moved to the bar.

Christine drew herself up and rolled her ball. This time she took out all but two pins. On the next roll, she made her first spare.

When she returned to her seat, Bear was watching her. "Nice pickup. By the way, if that creep is bothering you—"

"Oh no," she interrupted smoothly, "he was just trying to be helpful."

Christine's game continued to improve on each turn. When they were finished, Bear's score beat hers by a considerable margin, but she was satisfied that she'd bowled well enough not to embarrass herself. It had never been her goal to beat him, not at bowling anyway.

Bear sat back and studied her when they were finished. "You've played this game before." Not the game between them perhaps. There was still that air of competition between them, but it had nothing to do with bowling.

"I took a bowling class in college to fulfill one of my physical education requirements, since I never enjoyed the run-sweat-calisthenics type of P.E. courses. But it's been a while, and I forgot most of what I knew."

"You did okay." The corners of his mouth twitched slightly as he glanced at the bench where the tattooed man sat. "Of course, you got a little help from Schwarzenegger."

She grinned. "Arnold's cool, isn't he?"

He shook his head. She surprised the hell out of him. "To tell you the truth, I was hoping I wouldn't have to tangle with him just to preserve your honor."

Christine cocked her head. "Hey, give me a little credit. I *could* be cruising on a Harley about now."

Bear affected a look of mock outrage. "You're breaking my heart."

"Yeah, right." Christine slipped off her shoes, relieved to get the stinky things off her feet. "The only thing breaking your heart is I didn't turn and run the minute I walked into this place. Admit it, Malone."

He shrugged. "I'll admit I figured someone like you would turn her nose up at this place."

"Someone like me?" She shook her head. "But I didn't."

He looked at her a moment. If he were honest with himself, he'd have to concede that she had been a good sport. She'd passed the evening with an attitude of acceptance or, at least, an air of agreeable tolerance. The locals had approved of her, especially in the case of one who'd approved of her a little too well to suit him. "One evening doesn't prove anything. Anyone can be a good sport for a few hours."

A cagey look came into her eyes. "Right you are, Mr. Malone. Which, interestingly enough, brings us to the second half of our experiment."

Flipping off the console light, he began to untie his shoes. "Which is?"

She smiled. "I have two tickets to The Nutcracker next Friday night." She saw the painful grimace, but she ignored it. "I don't suppose you're interested."

She could barely hear his answer. "Is that that ballet crap?"

"Maybe we ought to get out of here." She batted her eyes. "I can't hear you very well. Your voice has turned kind of raspy. Must be all this smoke in here getting to you."

She slipped into her tennis shoes and headed to the counter to return the bowling shoes. Wordlessly, Bear rose and followed her. Outside on the sidewalk, she took his hand and dumped some cash into it.

"What's this?" he asked.

"For the shoes. I pay my own way."

"You're one pigheaded woman, Brighton."

Her brows lifted. "Why, it must *have* been the smoke. You seem to be in full voice now."

He reluctantly shoved the change into his pocket.

She glanced up at him under a moonlit sky. "Now, the ballet begins at eight. We'll have to allow driving time into the city, so how about I pick you up at six-thirty?"

Bear's brow was creased. It was obvious that his

first instinct was to refuse. He became aware that she was watching him, studying his expression, expecting a negative response.

He looked at her, and she could see the war going on in his brain.

He could see her smirk forming.

The phrase "I told you so" was on the tip of her tongue. She'd baited the hook and was waiting for him to take it.

"That's generous of you," he said noncommittally.

"Are you a fan of the ballet?" she asked. The game fish was circling warily. Now to wriggle the bait a bit. "I love ballet, and I rather thought you would too."

His smile was enigmatic. "Yeah, I am a patron of the arts."

Her tone was deceptively casual. "All of them?"

"With a few minor exceptions."

"Then I'd expect you would jump at the chance to see some of the finest guest professionals ever to come to San Francisco."

"I imagine those tickets set you back a pretty penny." For all he knew, she didn't have any tickets. Could be, she was just testing him. "I'd assume you'd want to take someone you really care about. Someone like the twerp, for instance."

She shook her head. "Actually, Percy's tastes are rather limited. He doesn't enjoy the ballet or the opera. Rock concerts are more his fare." Her eyes narrowed. "So how about it? Friday, six-thirty?"

Swallowing his pride, he drew his collar up closer. "My only concern is to keep this transaction equitable. Those tickets of yours probably cost big bucks. . . . The bowling was next to nothing in comparison."

She crossed her arms and tilted her head. "If it makes you feel better, the tickets are complimentary, a token from a grateful client who put my department in a bit of a crack last week." She almost had him. She could feel it. "I didn't pay a cent for them, so actually you're out more money than I, at this point."

He looked at her, defeated.

She could see his shoulders begin to sag. Time to set the hook. She shrugged. "Of course, if you'd rather not . . ."

"Next Friday?"

She nodded. He would balk about the day, but she had that one covered too. She could exchange her tickets for another night with one of the other employees who'd also received tickets. In just a matter of moments, she'd be the winner, he the loser. When he finally refused to attend the ballet on any night, she'd have him because then he'd have to admit that he was the snobbish one, the narrow-minded one, the one who was too threatened to appreciate tastes and backgrounds other than his own.

"Friday it is then." He straightened his back and summoned what looked like a genuine smile of enthusiasm. "I'd be happy to go to the ballet with you."

"What?" she croaked.

He glanced at the crisp, star-studded sky. "We better get you to your car, Christine. This night air is making you hoarse."

Taking her elbow, he guided her past a long row of motorcycles to her car. Her mind was racing.

What had gone wrong? She had been sure that he was about to refuse.

"Let me unlock your door," he offered. "You look shot."

She fumbled in her pocket for her keys. "I'll need directions to your place." If she pinned him down, she was sure that he'd still try to back out.

He patted his pockets. "I don't have anything to write on. Besides, if I don't see you at the house, I'll phone you sometime during the week and arrange a convenient place for us to meet."

He was stalling, she decided. "Perhaps we should leave at six-fifteen on Friday." She figured if he was hedging, she'd press her advantage. "Remember, we'll need to allow time for parking."

He smiled. Only then did she realize how close they were standing to each other, only then did she realize how searchingly his eyes were looking into hers.

She swallowed against a dry throat. Time to clarify her meaning, she thought. "Finding parking space in the city is always a challenge, you know."

He was looking at her so intently, his electric-blue eyes following the crimson blush as it moved up her cheeks. She had a sudden vision of the two of them inside her car, clutching each other wantonly, kissing passionately, while her car windows steamed up and misted over. Surely, he wasn't thinking the same thing! The very prospect that he might be reading her mind made her want to curl up and die.

The corners of his mouth twitched as if he were enjoying her discomfort. "You know," he said, "I'll need your keys to unlock your door."

She quickly dug to the bottom of her pocket and grabbed her keys. She slapped them into his open palm. He nodded and turned to open her door.

"Well, thanks for the evening," she said quickly, swinging into the driver's seat. "I had fun."

He leaned on the open door and stared at her, his look penetrating, assessing. "Yes," he said slowly, "I think you actually did."

As the irony hit her, the corners of her mouth lifted. "Well, don't sound so disappointed."

"I'm not." Strangely enough it was true. Although the evening had not gone the way he'd figured it would, she'd had a good time, and so had he. However, that did nothing to change his opinion. He felt certain that her feelings of superiority would surface sooner or later.

She glanced at her watch. "It's late, I better be going."

He closed her door. With a wave, he stepped away.

She shifted into reverse and backed out of the space. Shifting into first, she let herself glance at him one more time before pulling out. As she drove away, she felt a letdown. He had agreed to go to the ballet with her when she could have sworn that he was on the verge of refusing.

Well, Friday was a whole week away. It wouldn't surprise her one bit if he contacted her during the coming days to express his regrets. Some convenient reason would pop up. She was certain that some time before six-fifteen Friday night she'd hear Bear Malone tell her thanks, but no thanks.

However, if he called with some lame ruse, they'd both know it, and she would point it out to him. Then he'd still have to admit that he was the snob. A smile of triumph spread across her face. He'd call with some half-baked excuse. Nothing short of a death in the family would serve as a plausible explanation to get him out of The Nutcracker.

Five

"How *awful*. Were you and your uncle close?" Christine grinned as she cradled her office phone closer to her ear.

"No," Bear explained. "Actually, I had met him only once. My father's family never kept in touch. My sister tells me that it was a heart attack. Fortunately, he didn't suffer."

Christine sobered. He had her on this one. "Well, today is Thursday." It occurred to her that it would be rude and insensitive for her to suggest that his uncle's death was an excuse for him to call off going to the ballet with her. "I can understand why you would prefer a rain check on the ballet tomorrow night."

"That's not why I called. I've been in Colorado this week, helping my sister Annie with the arrangements and attending the funeral. I thought if you'd gone to work on the house one evening, you might wonder why I wasn't there."

"I've been working late, so I haven't had a chance to swing by the house this week." Christine felt a pang of guilt for even suspecting that Bear would use a death in the family as a convenient excuse to get out of going to a ballet. "I'm really sorry about your uncle." Suddenly, their challenge seemed rather petty anyway. "Hey, I don't blame you for wanting to skip going out after the week you've been through. I'll think I'll give the tickets away and work late tomorrow night." That would be a more productive use of her time anyway.

"Christine, I wasn't calling to cancel our plans. Actually, it would probably do me good to go out, get my mind off things. I was calling to suggest that it would probably be more convenient for you to pick me up at the little restaurant where we had lunch a few weeks ago. It's an easy walk from my place, and that way you won't have to drive the BMW down the sandy road."

"Oh." She sat in stunned silence for a moment. Just when she thought she had him figured out, he seemed to throw her a curve.

"By the way, could we meet at six o'clock instead of at six-fifteen like we agreed before?" he asked.

"Sure," she murmured, "six o'clock."

"See you then."

"Yeah . . . then . . ." She sat listening to the buzzing dial tone, wondering what was going on. He'd moved their meeting time up fifteen minutes when he had the perfect excuse to break their date—*their date?* Correction, she thought. These evenings together were definitely *not* dates. They could better be described as experiments, part of a mutual challenge, which she was beginning to think was not going to prove anything anyway.

Oh well, she thought, raking her fingers through

her hair. She was swamped at work and since it didn't appear she'd be working late tomorrow night, she'd better get busy. She heaved a long sigh. Putting in sixty-hour workweeks, week in and week out, was taking its toll. The life of an energetic, up-and-coming executive was not all it was cracked up to be. It wasn't so glamorous putting in long days only to feel used rather than appreciated, she decided. She'd felt pure elation when she'd landed this plum position. Now she wasn't so thrilled.

When had this sense of dissatisfaction emerged? she wondered. Her mind rolled back over the past few months. It had begun when she had started working on renovating run-down houses, a civic project she truly loved. That was shortly before she'd met Bear Malone. Could he have anything to do with her malaise?

"Totally ridiculous," she muttered. So where had it come from, this restless feeling that there had to be more to living than pouring yourself into a company that wouldn't remember your name a week after you died? "Good grief, how morbid," she grumbled. No, just tired of the rat race, she thought. *I'm just bone tired,* she decided, before reluctantly admitting that perhaps Bear's call about his uncle's death might have contributed to the downward turn of her emotions.

On Friday, at six o'clock sharp, Christine pulled into the designated meeting spot. She smiled with the memory of the day they had first met. They certainly had not taken to each other right away. She wasn't sure they even liked each other now, though she'd have to admit there was more to the man than she'd first thought. By her assessment, he was generous, bighearted, and unselfish, as well as stubborn, bullheaded, and opinionated.

She switched off the motor and scanned the interior of the restaurant through the plate glass windows. She didn't see him among the diners, and he was the sort of person who stood out in a crowd. She glanced down the narrow, sandy road leading to the beach and recognized Bear walking up the road dressed in a work shirt and jeans, carrying a paper grocery bag.

Her eyes widened. Will he *ever* stand out in the crowd tonight, she thought.

He waved at her as he drew near. The chambray shirt looked clean, as did the jeans, and he was freshly shaven. In the late-afternoon sun, droplets of water glistened in his dark wavy hair from a recent shower.

Well, she decided, at least he looks neat and clean. And wasn't that what her mother had said really counted. "Christine," she could hear her mother's voice inside her head as she'd heard it a hundred times before, "it doesn't matter what a person wears as long as he's neat and clean. It isn't what a person wears that counts, anyway, but what's inside his heart matters a whole lot."

"Well, Mama," Christine murmured, "I guess in that case you'd approve of Bear Malone."

"Hi," he greeted with an engaging smile as he opened the door and swung into the passenger seat. He dropped the sack between his feet. She sincerely hoped it didn't contain a thermos and a lunch box. The last thing she wanted was another spill in her car, or worse yet did he plan to munch his way through the ballet? With a sinking heart, she realized that if he did that, she'd die.

She mustered a small smile. "Hi, yourself."

He seemed genuinely glad to see her as he looked her over. "Say, you sure look nice."

"Oh, thanks," she said automatically. Her gaze dropped down to her ebony velvet suit with the rhinestone buttons that winked in the rays of the setting sun.

When she glanced back at Bear, he was eyeing her legs once more.

What a pair we make, she thought. There won't be another couple at the ballet tonight who was more mismatched. It suddenly occurred to her that maybe Bear had dressed this way just to make that point. Maybe he thought she was such a snob that she would refuse to take him to the ballet because he was in work clothes. That would be a perfect method for him to win their little bet; Agree to go to the ballet, then show up inappropriately dressed. If she didn't take him, then she proved his worst suspicions, and he would have won the challenge.

That had to be his plan, she decided. And she had to admit it was a dandy.

Her lips curved into a subtle smile. Well, your little plan is going to fail, Mr. Malone, she thought to herself. I'll take you to the city, to the ballet, to the elegant backstage party afterward, even to the little coffeehouse, and it won't bother me what you wear or how you behave, not one little bit.

She fired up the engine and pulled out of the parking lot. "Nice evening for a drive to the city," she said in a light conversational tone, determined that he would not detect even a trace of irritation in her demeanor.

After a couple of miles, he checked the digital time display on the dash. "Since we've gotten an early start, I hope you won't mind if we make one quick stop."

"Well, I don't know," she said, a bit confused.

"It'll only take a minute. Turn at the next corner and pull into that parking lot over there." He was pointing to a little strip of stores just off the highway.

She flicked on her right blinker. "No problem." She wouldn't give him the satisfaction of unsettling her again. It appeared that since his wardrobe trick had backfired, he was going to needle her with a series of annoying delays. Fine, she thought to herself, nothing says we have to arrive before the curtain goes up.

She turned onto the small parking lot and slowed to a stop, unsure where he'd want her to park.

"Right here is just fine," he said as he hopped out. "You can keep the motor running. I'll be back in a jiffy." He closed the door.

"Yeah, right," she muttered as he trotted off. "Don't you ever get tired of giving orders?" she demanded as he disappeared around the corner. As an act of defiance, she switched off the motor.

Leaning back against the headrest, she closed her eyes and pictured herself walking on the beach, the waves rolling in, bathing her feet, making her footprints behind her disappear. It was a scene she often conjured up when she needed to relax.

She lost track of time during her meditation, but her eyes popped open when she heard the passenger door open.

"Sorry, I didn't mean to startle you."

Her mouth dropped open as she watched Bear

drop into the seat beside her, dressed in a formal black tuxedo.

The tops of his work boots were sticking out of the grocery sack he set on the floor. She glanced at the fine black leather dress shoes he was wearing and realized that he had probably brought them along in the bag. With a flip of his wrist, he tossed his work clothes into the back seat.

"Since I was out of town most of the week, I didn't have a chance to get by the cleaners for my tux. Hope you didn't mind making the stop."

She sat there speechless, staring at him. He smiled at her then, and he looked so rakishly handsome that for an instant she forgot to breathe. "Hey, we better get a move on. Don't want to be late, do we?"

She shook her head. "No," she said dazedly. "No, we don't." She turned the key and started the engine.

"Something wrong?" he asked. "You look kind of pale."

"No, I'm fine." She pulled out onto the highway. *Why is it,* she wondered, *every time I think I've got him pegged, he does a one eighty on me?*

She could have sworn that he'd called her at work yesterday to cancel their plans, especially since he had an excuse she couldn't deny without seeming hopelessly inconsiderate. Then he met her wearing clothes that she felt certain were deliberately chosen to provoke a rude objection from her. And now he's acting as though he's enthused about attending a ballet, to the point of showing concern about their arriving late. The man doesn't even wear a watch for heaven's sake! Since when did he care about being on time? Was he messing with her mind, or was she misjudging him all the time? A long silence stretched between them while she tried to sort out the incongruities.

They headed north up the coastline where the cliffs rose up out of the sea and the wind blew stronger, sending the waves onto the rocks in a shower of spray.

Bear broke into her thoughts. "I like it up here. Fewer people, a slower pace."

She nodded. "Sometimes I drive up to Stinson Beach, just to get away from it all."

"I imagine you get a little tired of the crowds where you work."

She shrugged. "I used to think it was all so exciting."

"And now?" His tone remained casual, but he turned his head to study her profile in the long evening shadows.

"Sometimes I wonder what it's all about, if it's worth it in the long run."

"I suppose that depends on what you want."

She stared at the road and felt the urge to change the subject. He was asking her questions she had not dared to ask herself. "What about you? Don't you get a little lonely working solo so much of the time?"

"Sometimes. But then if you don't have a crew, you don't have anyone talking back."

She glanced at him then. "Why do I get the impression you like to give the orders?"

He turned and looked at the strip of windswept beach that momentarily broke into view. "I guess I get a little bossy sometimes."

She nodded. "I think you could say that."

He chuckled. "It seems to be a fault we have in common."

Ironically enough, it seemed to be one of the few

traits they had in common. Christine nodded. "That's us. Two chiefs, no Indians."

"Perhaps we need to recruit a couple of work crews. Doesn't seem to work too well, the two of us trying to boss each other."

She laughed. To her surprise, she discovered that at times like this he could be humble too. "I think I've rounded up enough to make one crew. It'll take me a while to come up with enough people for two crews."

"One crew would be a big improvement. When could they start?"

She smiled at the interest in his voice. "Would tomorrow at nine be soon enough?"

"I think I could handle that." He looked at her with increased admiration. "Are they skilled?"

"Skilled? In their professions, yes. In home building, no."

"Oh."

"But they're bright and willing to do anything you ask of them."

"Then they'll do fine."

They arrived in time to find a parking space without much hassle. After she locked the doors and slipped the key into her satin handbag, Bear took her elbow and shortened his stride to match her pace as she clipped along in her suede pumps. She couldn't have asked for a more genteel escort as they moved down the sidewalk and stepped inside the auditorium.

She glanced around at the dazzling interior and the beautiful people. As an usher guided them to their seats, heads turned their way. At that moment, Christine felt like Cinderella out on the town with the handsome prince.

Bear remained alert throughout the performance.

He neither dozed, complained, nor shifted around in his seat. When the crowd rose for a standing ovation at the end, he reached for Christine's elbow to guide her to her feet.

Her worst fears about his possible behavior seemed groundless. She began to wonder if she was becoming paranoid.

She glanced up at him. "We've been invited backstage for a party with the performers. Would you mind attending?"

For an instant, his brow furrowed. Then his face brightened. "Why would I mind? Let's go."

She wondered if his face was contorted in concentration or consternation. Was he as willing as he seemed, or was he pretending that he didn't mind? Again, she found herself perplexed by his response.

They made their way through a dark and dreary passage, then followed party noises into a bright, colorful room. Bear lifted two glasses of champagne from a waiter's tray and handed one to Christine.

While they sipped, they watched the ballerinas flutter from group to group, their long filmy skirts swirling like moth wings. A couple of the male dancers began to circulate through the crowd, shaking hands and accepting compliments.

A male dancer still wearing his satin tunic and thin, white tights took Christine's hand, kissed her on the cheek, and smiled into her eyes. She smiled back. "We enjoyed the performance, Henri," she said. "It was lovely, and of course you were magnificent."

"Thanks, darling," the young man said.

Feeling Bear's eyes move back and forth between her and the dancer, Christine turned to

Bear. "I'd like to introduce Henri Simone. This is Bear Malone." To Bear's inquisitive stare, Christine added, "Henri and I met at a party."

As Henri and Bear shook hands, a middle-aged woman joined their group, whom Henri introduced as the manager of the company. She kept her eyes on Bear, her gaze taking in his narrow hips, pausing where the black cummerbund lay flat against his waist, then moving up the crisp white tucked shirt to the breadth of his shoulders. "My, my . . ." she said appreciatively, sliding to his side and reaching up to squeeze his bicep.

Bear's dark brows lowered ominously. But unaffected by his response, she grinned up at him. "And so strong too," she added. "My, my, would I ever like to see you in tights. If you ever want to audition—"

"Let's go, Christine," Bear interrupted gruffly.

Henri spun away, laughing as he went, taking the woman with him. Christine couldn't keep from chuckling too. Bear nailed her with a suspicious glare as if she were an accomplice to the scene rather than an observer.

"I suppose you find that amusing?" he demanded.

"Afraid so." She tried to look serious but had trouble managing it. "If you could've seen the expression on your face when she suggested—"

"Okay." He raised both hands abruptly. "I catch your drift." He glanced around the room while his fingers hooked into his collar and tugged at it. "Does it seem awfully warm to you in here?"

"A little." Whether he'd enjoyed it or not, he'd managed to sit through the ballet quietly. She could see, however, that the party was obviously making him uncomfortable. She glanced around and shrugged. "Well, we could stay here for a while or . . ."

"Or?" He looked at her, and his brows shot up.

She interpreted his reaction as pure, undisguised hope. He'd proved that he could be a pretty good actor, until now. It was obvious to her that he was only enduring this party. She wondered if she should put him out of his misery or let him suffer awhile longer. "Or . . . we could go to a little coffeehouse nearby where people sometimes grab a bite and chat after a performance."

He couldn't hide his relief. "Now that you mention it, I'm starved. Been a long time since lunch."

"You didn't have an afternoon snack?"

"I don't remember it if I did."

She shook her head. The man could eat a mountain of food and be hungry in an hour. Her glance drifted down his frame, all muscle, slim and strong. She sighed. The man could eat for two and still look great.

"Well, Bear, if you're sure you don't mind leaving this wonderful party . . ."

He had her elbow and was guiding her to the door. "I'll live."

They walked the few blocks to the coffeehouse. As they stepped inside the door they halted, exchanging glances. The long waiting line for a table was backed almost out to the sidewalk. A girl in a long black dress, carrying a clipboard, walked up to them. "How many?" she asked.

"Two," Christine replied. "How long is the wait?"

The girl ran her gaze down three quarters of the page. "I'd say it'll be forty-five minutes to an hour."

Christine glanced up at Bear. His lips had formed a tight line, and she knew that he'd never last that long. She turned back to the girl and shook her head. "No, thanks. We'll try you another time."

The girl was already moving to a couple who'd opened the door behind them. Back on the sidewalk, Christine glanced at him. "Want to try someplace else?"

"Are you in the mood for seafood and a slower pace?"

She smiled. "I'm game."

"Then let's head back down the coast. I know a little out-of-the-way place."

She fell into step beside him. "Can you hold out that long?"

He nodded. "It'll be worth the wait."

An hour later, they pulled into a lot graveled with crushed seashells. "This is the place," Bear said, helping her out from behind the steering wheel. "Best calamari on the coast."

"Calamari?" she asked.

He looked at her in shock. "You haven't eaten calamari?"

"I arrived here only a few months ago. I don't remember seeing it on menus in Des Moines."

"Gee," he said incredulously, "sounds more like you arrived a few hours ago. You're not a California girl if you haven't tasted calamari."

She shrugged. "So teach me."

He cupped her elbow. "I plan to."

The restaurant was hardly more than a beach hut. Because of the late hour, there were only a few patrons. They sat at a wooden picnic table and looked out through an open window at the breakers rolling in the moonlight. It was a world away from the sophistication of the city, a safe haven. Christine inhaled the breeze off the ocean, and when she exhaled she could feel her cares begin to melt away.

She turned to find Bear watching her from the corner of his eye. "You're relaxing," he said. "It's good to see you that way. You usually seem so tense."

"It shows?" She preferred to think that she kept her stress under control, but lately it had seemed relentless.

"Oh yes, it shows."

They were served baskets of deep-fried calamari between halves of crusty French bread, curly fries, and frosty mugs of beer. The food was fresh and hot and delicious. Christine picked up her thick sandwich and took a tentative bite.

"Well," Bear asked, "what's the verdict?"

"Mmmm, wonderful."

"I thought you'd enjoy it here."

They ate in contented silence, watching the frothy waves chase one another to shore. When she'd nearly finished her meal, Christine glanced at Bear. "What is this calamari anyway? I don't think I've ever tasted anything quite like it."

"But you do like it?" he asked.

She nodded. "Sure."

"Perhaps I'll tell you later."

She didn't like him making decisions for her. "What's the big deal? If you won't tell me now, I'll ask the waitress."

He looked at her thoughtfully. "Okay. Actually, it's deep-fried . . . squid."

"Squid?" She looked at the last of the sandwich in her hands in disbelief. "Okay, what is it really?" She lifted her inquisitive gaze to study the frank expression in his eyes, the straight, no-nonsense set of his mouth, the long, determined jaw. *Oh no,* she surmised, *he's telling me the truth.* Her face fell as she laid the rest of her sandwich in his basket.

"Ah, come on. Surely you aren't swearing off calamari just because you know what it is."

"I'll eat it again." She didn't want to look like a pansy.

"You will?" he asked with a lingering doubt in his voice.

"Sure." She shrugged. "I'll just let myself forget what it is before I order it again."

He shook his head. "I wouldn't buy it from anyone else. But somehow coming from you, that makes perfect sense." There was a trace of affection in his voice.

She glanced up at him with the look of a question in her eyes.

He helped her push back their bench from the table. "Come on. Why don't we walk off this meal before we start back?"

She looked out at the beach. Since she'd moved to California, she'd experienced too few moments with the feel of sand between her toes. "You're on."

Outside, they kicked off their shoes like children. While he removed his socks, she slipped around the corner and slipped off her stockings. When she came back, she walked past him to the patio table where they'd left their shoes.

The corners of his mouth twitched as he sat on a bench, watching her tuck her stockings discreetly into her suede pumps. For all her worldly sophistication, she really was modest.

He stood and extended his palm. She slipped her hand into his, and they struck off, sinking to their ankles in the deep sand. As they moved closer to the sea, the sand became harder packed.

It felt damp and cool, glistening in the moonlight. With the breeze ruffling their hair, they began to walk slower. Christine stopped and faced the surf, listening to the waves slap the sand, creep in, and whisper to her before rolling out again.

She inched closer to the water's edge, her toes curling into the wet sand, but he hung back, still holding her hand, their arms stretching out straight.

"That's close enough," he warned.

She glanced over her shoulder. "Oh, what's the fun if you don't get a little wet?"

"You'll be sorry."

"It'll be worth it." She edged out further to watch the surf bubble over her toes. She sucked in her breath at the first icy sting.

"Enjoying yourself?"

"Yes," she responded decisively. "What's the good of coming so close and never knowing the feel of it? Might as well watch the surf on television if you're not willing to get your feet wet."

He shook his head. Why did everything always become a challenge between them? He made his decision and shrugged. After all, he'd been wet and cold often enough, one more time wouldn't matter.

He squeezed her hand as he waded out a step beyond her to stand where the surf rolled over his ankles.

She looked up at him and grinned. "Isn't it great?"

"Exhilarating," he said, gazing at the sparkle in her eyes. Her enthusiasm was infectious. Despite her elegant suit, she was an Iowa girl enthralled with the California surf.

"I've missed something, haven't I?" she said softly. "Too much time at the office."

He returned her smile. She was more spontaneous than he'd imagined. "You have a crazy streak, you know."

She gave a quick laugh. "I should hope so. When you describe people like me, we sound deadly dull."

They were standing shoulder to shoulder, facing the sea, when he added, "You're anything but dull."

She looked up at him, her face pale, her dark eyes luminous. His deep-set eyes were in shadow, and his smile had disappeared. In its place was a searching scrutiny. He looked as if he were trying to look inside her.

The breeze softened, and the atmosphere between them changed. Something about him was pulling at her with a magnetic strength, much the way the tide was tugging the sand beneath her feet.

She felt a need to diffuse the tension building between them as she tried to swallow the lump in her throat. She was going to have to quit teasing this man. He was not likely to back down from the lightest dare. She was accustomed to boys like Percy, who would have ignored her taunts and abandoned her at the water's edge.

Her toes were freezing, but she wasn't about to admit that now. As the surf rolled out, she waded out farther until she stood a foot beyond Bear Malone. She figured she'd feel more comfortable if she put a little distance between them. She looked at the sea. The wavelets seemed to be gathering momentum.

"You know," he began, "if you can believe what

you hear, they say if you count the waves as they wash ashore, every seventh one is much bigger than the others."

Her eyes grew wide. "Surely, you don't believe such nonsense." It seemed that the waves were looming, drawing themselves up, their ruffled white manes glowing under the moon.

"We'll see," he said matter-of-factly.

Her mouth dropped open as the wave ahead seemed to poise for an instant. The crash was louder than before as it tumbled toward her, and raced to the beach.

Her hand clenched his tightly as the surf consumed her feet, her ankles, her calves, and licked at her knees before it rolled away.

"Well, I don't know about you," he began in a wry tone, "but it's a much fuller experience for me to stand out here where I can get thoroughly soaked."

"Oh, you," she muttered as she turned to drag him toward shore. She glared up at him. "Admit it," she demanded, "you had fun too."

He sighed as he reached into his hip pocket. "Yeah, I had fun. I especially enjoyed the look on your face when that seventh wave got so much larger." Extracting a white handkerchief, he knelt on one knee. "Your foot, madame."

"What?" She rested her hand on his shoulder for support as he pulled her foot forward to wipe away the cold moisture. "You don't need to do that. I'll be fine."

"Sure you will," he said, ignoring her protests. "You won't be much help on the house if you're home nursing a cold." He unceremoniously grasped her other foot and dried it. Straightening, he stood and swiped some of the wet sand off his feet with the wet handkerchief.

"I won't catch cold."

"No," he agreed, "if it's not on your schedule, you probably won't permit it to happen."

She slanted a glance up at him. "What's that supposed to mean?"

He shrugged. "I guess I was thinking that even if you got sick, you'd probably be too bullheaded to admit it."

They were facing each other toe to toe. She playfully punched his arm, then shook out her fingers as if the encounter with his firm bicep had injured her knuckles. "My, my," she said appreciatively, imitating the manager of the ballet company, "and so strong too." She placed her palm on his broad chest and smiled up at him. "Would I ever like to see you in a pair of tights. You know if you ever decide to audition . . ."

"All you have to do is ask." He made a decision to silence her in the most expedient and interesting way possible. Without warning, he cupped his hands over her shoulders.

She told herself that he must have taken hold of her to balance himself. She knew better when he hauled her against him. Her breathing stopped as his head lowered. She had meant to tease him, provoke him perhaps, but she hadn't anticipated this sort of reaction.

His lips were warm as they met hers firmly. She told herself to resist, to push herself away, but there was something intoxicating about the way he gathered her close, about the way his lips moved over hers persuasively, seductively. Beneath her palms on his chest, she could feel his heartbeat grow stronger, resonating through her fingertips.

Yearning for more, she leaned against him. For such a strong, powerful man, she found it surprising that the touch of his lips on hers, the caress of his hands on her shoulders were so gentle.

His fingertips fanned out over her back in light circles that sent tingles down her spine. When he lifted his head, she stood still with her eyes tightly closed, regretting that their kiss was over so soon. A moment later she felt his lips brushing over her eyes and her cheeks.

An aching began to build inside her as she waited, hoping that his lips would return to hers. Unconsciously, she lifted her head, inviting his kiss. She was not disappointed.

This time his lips were more demanding as they opened, drawing hers apart. His tongue stroked and teased in a delicious way as her fingers toyed with the hair that spilled over his collar. Her hands smoothed up over his shoulders as she strained closer.

A voice inside her warned that all of this was unwise, that she would regret it later, that it would change things between them, that this was not part of their bargain. Or was it? With a flash of uninvited clarity, she suspected that this was what their challenge had been about all along.

The tension between them, the nerves chafing, the competitive edge—perhaps it had been amplified by the growing awareness between them, the increasing attraction. Was that what they meant about opposites attracting? She had told herself all along that the two of them were combating each other because of their differences. Had she been kidding herself? Apparently so, she conceded silently.

Laying her head on his chest, she closed her

eyes. Here she could hear the roar of the surf and the steady pounding of his heart. Here she could feel the pull of the tide and the pull of attraction between them. Inside her, a war raged between what she wanted to do and what she thought she ought to do.

He sensed her hesitation. With a pang of regret, he felt an invisible wall going up between them. It occurred to him that she had started thinking again, probably reminding herself that he wasn't in her league. He liked her better when she let herself go on her feelings alone.

Releasing his hold on her, he watched as she took a step back and stood facing him, drawing in a deep, steadying breath.

He looked at her for a long moment, trying to resign himself to the fact that she obviously didn't want to let herself get carried away with a nobody like him. That sudden realization bothered him more than he ever could have imagined.

"Come on," he said gruffly as he turned around. "It's getting late. It's time we called it a night."

Six

The following morning Christine dabbed discreetly at her nose with a tissue as she sat in her car in the driveway of the run-down house. After awakening with a sore throat and a stuffy head, she'd remembered Bear's warning to her the night before that if she got wet in the freezing surf, she'd catch cold. She had refused to listen to him then, and the last thing she wanted to hear from his lips now was that he told her so.

Desperate for relief, she'd risen before dawn to rummage through her medicine chest. The only thing she'd found was a liquid nighttime cold remedy with an expiration date from the last century. Two aspirin and a steamy shower had cleared her head, but the chilly morning fog was making her throat feel raw.

Bear had the lights on inside the house, and she sat for a moment, watching him carry boxes from room to room. She glanced at her watch. The volunteer work crew was due in an hour. It occurred to her that if she waited for them to arrive before going inside, Bear might be distracted enough not to notice her condition. The coward's way out, she admonished herself.

If she were honest with herself, she'd have to admit the real cause for her hesitation was that she didn't want to face him. She wasn't avoiding him because she had the sniffles. The vivid memory of their kiss the night before was the main reason she was reluctant to go inside.

During a nearly sleepless night, she'd tried to blame her response to him on everything from beer to moonlight. In the opaque light of dawn, she found it harder to kid herself. She'd been kissed before, but no one had affected her the way Bear Malone had.

He had effortlessly evoked needs and longings that she'd prefer not to know. The feelings he'd elicited had returned to claw at her in the middle of the night. She didn't need such distractions in her life. They would result in nothing but trouble.

Instinctively, she'd known all along to avoid him. Without being told, she'd felt a premonition that if she didn't keep her distance, he'd complicate her life. To make matters worse, he had mistaken her defense mechanism for snobbery.

From some misguided impulse, she'd felt it necessary to prove him wrong about that, and so between them a challenge had formed, each determined to reveal the other as the perpetrator of snap judgments. She was beginning to suspect that they were both to some degree the victims of sterotyping.

As she climbed out of her car, the musty odor of moldy soil made her nose twitch. Breathing through her mouth to avoid provoking a sneeze, she strode to the house. When she stepped inside, the smell of fresh-cut lumber was almost too much. Normally, she loved the woody fragrance, but today she swallowed thickly to stifle a cough. She discreetly popped a honey-lemon lozenge into her mouth before shrugging out of her jacket.

"Well, hello."

She jumped at the sound of his voice and spun to face him. His wry tone and the way he looked at her with one brow cocked told her that he had not expected her to show up.

The sun was trying unsuccessfully to penetrate the haze, casting a sickly, yellowish glow over the room. She stood facing him, feeling again the fresh ache of rejection she'd experienced when he'd abruptly turned on his heel and trudged down the beach away from her nearly eight hours ago.

Fog crept through the open living room windows in slinky coils as she endured the same awkward silence she'd experienced on their ride back to town. He'd insisted that she let him off at the restaurant where she'd picked him up. It had been closed by then, and Bear Malone had disappeared into the mist as soon as he'd closed the car door.

She realized how foolish she'd been to let herself hope that he might behave as if last night had never happened. She decided to duck any confrontation. She didn't feel up to one today, so she opted for a distraction. "Did the doors arrive?"

He nodded. "They were on the porch when I got here."

She glanced around and spotted the four new doors where he'd leaned them against the far wall. Hurrying across the room to take a closer look, she was relieved for an excuse to put some distance between them.

She leaned to touch them, first one then another. "Can we use them?" she asked. "You know Brosman Construction was glad to donate these because they were blemished and couldn't use them as first quality."

"They'll do. I think we can hang them so the dings won't be noticeable."

"Good." She turned to face him. "Bill Brosman promised to let me have these doors weeks ago, but he kept forgetting to have someone put them on a delivery truck when it was headed this way. You have to get things when people are in the mood to get rid of them." Her eyes widened. "You know if we had our own delivery truck, we could pick up donations right away."

Bear's glance flicked to the paint cans across the room, and he started toward them. She frowned. It wasn't like him to walk off during a conversation. Her gaze followed him as he grabbed three handles in each hand, hoisted the six gallons of paint, and headed for the kitchen. "Bear, I'm talking to you."

"I can hear you and work at the same time."

She found herself trailing after him. "As I was saying, if we had a delivery truck we'd get lots more in donations. You have to show up when the getting is good." She watched him set the cans on the floor and pry the lid off one of them. "We've had some wonderful things promised to the project slip away because they weren't picked up immediately." Though he didn't appear to be listening, she continued. "Once word gets out that something is free, employees and relatives jump in and help themselves. That leaves us out in the cold. Bear? Are you listening?"

He was stirring the paint and shaking his head. "I don't know what we're going to do with this."

She crossed the room and looked at the paint. "What's wrong with it?"

He gave her a droll look. "Passion-pink?"

She shrugged. "Can't we add some white or something and tone it down?"

He released a long breath. "We'll have to."

"See? That's my point. When that paint was offered to us, we could've had our choice of colors. By the time they got around to bringing it to us, passion-pink was all that was left."

Replacing the paint lid, he murmured, "I think I heard a car in the driveway."

She was turning toward the front door with the suspicion that he was trying to get rid of her when she heard the knock. Through the window, she spotted a familiar sleek cap of black hair and felt a rush of joy as she threw the door open wide. "Come in, Sarah."

Christine grabbed her friend and hugged her. She hadn't realized how much she'd missed seeing her.

Sarah hugged her back. "How long has it been since I've seen you?"

Christine sighed. "Too long."

Sarah leaned back to peer into her friend's face. "I can't catch you at the office. You're always out in the plant somewhere. At your apartment, I get your answering machine. Do you ever go home?"

"Just to sleep and change. You'll have to come here to catch up on our visiting." Christine pulled her friend into the room and raised her arms. "Well, what do you think?" She held her breath, her eyes bright with anticipation. Surely, she thought, Sarah will recognize the potential and feel inspired, just as she had the first time she'd walked into this place.

Sarah ignored the surroundings when she saw Bear wander into the room. "Impressive," she said succinctly.

Christine turned to glance over her shoulder. Sarah was not usually sarcastic and that was a more enthusiastic response than one would expect to the run-down appearance of this house. "Oh, Sarah, it doesn't look like much now, but this place is going to be gorgeous."

Sarah glanced at Christine and murmured under her breath, "The view is already improving, if you catch my drift." The speculative gleam in Sarah's eyes was unmistakable.

Christine followed Sarah's gaze across the room to where Bear was standing in the kitchen doorway, watching them. Sarah whispered, "Who's the hunk?"

Christine's breath caught in her throat and before she could stop it, she was seized by a fit of coughing. Sarah patted her back until Christine could control the spasm. "Gee, you better take something for that."

Christine cleared her throat and blinked away the moisture in her eyes. "It's nothing," she managed to say in a strangled voice.

Bear crossed the room with a few quick strides and tipped his head to study Christine's face with a look of concern. "I think she must have caught a cold."

"I bet she needs time to adjust to our damp ocean air."

"Or our damp ocean water as the case may be," he said, raising a brow accusingly.

Christine hated it when people talked about her

in her presence as if she weren't there. Her mother had frequently embarrassed her in front of her friends by talking with them about her. Like then, it sounded detached and condescending.

"I'm perfectly fine," she croaked.

Sarah extended her hand to Bear. "I'm Sarah Chetter."

Bear wiped his palm on his jeans before taking her hand. "Bear Malone."

Sarah gave his hand a brief, firm shake. "Glad to meet you, Bear," she said, her dark eyes lighting with mischief. "Christine has told me so many wonderful things about you."

Christine's mouth dropped open, and she looked hard at her friend. What was Sarah doing? She had never mentioned Bear to her.

Bear's brows lifted in what looked like surprise. "Has she?" he asked, with that familiar hint of mocking challenge in his voice.

Christine cleared her throat audibly. "I believe the wonderful things I mentioned to you were about the potential in this house."

"Ah yes, the house." Sarah let her gaze roam the room.

Christine studied her friend. Never had she known Sarah Chetter to confuse the facts. Her mind was as sharp as they came. "I've told you that Sarah is a public defender."

"Interesting," Bear commented.

Christine continued. "We met at the gym the first week I arrived in California. I told her if she joined us she could get a good workout here and be involved with something worthwhile at the same time."

"There's plenty to do," Bear agreed, gesturing with his paint stick.

Sarah's quick eyes moved back and forth between Bear and Christine, missing nothing. "I've been looking for something worthwhile to do with my leisure time, something I could do with my hands to help me forget my clients for a while."

Christine nodded. This was the friend she knew. In Sarah's daily life, winning and losing were everything. If she overlooked something, a defendant could be condemned. Sometimes it happened no matter what she did. Christine knew that the pressures were enormous, so sometimes to relieve the stress, they joked about it—gallows humor. "Sarah tells me when she's had a bad day, it usually means somebody's about to embark upon a career of making license plates."

"So you can see that I need an outlet."

Bear shrugged as he walked back into the kitchen, with the two women following him. "This place can keep you as busy as you want to be."

Sarah leaned to peek at the paint Bear had mixed in an old saucepan. "Oh, I like that shade. Mauve, isn't it?"

Christine shifted to look at the pale paint that moments ago had seemed so vivid. Her brows lifted as she glanced up at Bear.

His eyes smiled at Christine, their blue depths warm with amusement. "Mauve, it is."

"How did you get that color?" Christine asked. "Wasn't it hot pink before?"

"Blended in a pint of white and a touch of blue." He handed the saucepan to Christine. "You can start painting the nursery." It was the smallest of the three bedrooms upstairs. He handed Sarah a couple of new brushes and a roller set.

Christine grabbed a handful of paint rags and tucked them under her arm. "I guess you finished spackling and sanding the walls up there."

"Yesterday," he said.

Sarah seemed to be watching their exchange with interest when Christine glanced at her. "Ready to start?"

Sarah nodded. "Let's hit it. The others won't be here for a while yet."

The two women went upstairs. After Christine rolled the first strokes of color on the wall, she looked at Sarah. "I hope the family that moves in here has a little girl."

Sarah smiled. "I think he likes you. A lot."

Christine rolled her eyes. "I think you've been down at the courthouse too long. Your perceptions of the real world are way off."

"You don't like him?" Sarah's tone was casual.

Christine avoided the question. "Believe me, he's a major pain."

"Interesting." Sarah dipped her brush into the saucepan. "Part of my job is to sniff out the truth."

"Don't take this personally, but stop the psychoanalysis, okay?" Christine slapped a roller of paint on the wall. "He's one bullheaded man in more ways than I care to explain. It boils down to one simple fact: He's a major pain."

Sarah chuckled. "Honey, you've got it bad."

Christine squared her shoulders defensively. "I don't know what you mean by that. I'm stuck cochairing this project with a man who's certain he's always right, who believes I'm the yuppie of the year here to make a few points to impress my boss, who's sure that I'm destined for the Forbes list or bust."

"Listen, honey, I've been in the presence of towering egos, and it wasn't a clash of egos I just witnessed downstairs. To be perfectly candid, it was a case of colossal magnetism."

"Give me a break. You've been writing too many closing arguments to the jury. You are out of touch."

"Okay, okay," Sarah said, disbelief evident in her singsong tone, "whatever you say."

While Sarah applied careful brush strokes below the windowsill, Christine vigorously stirred up the paint with the stick. She told herself that her frustration stemmed from Sarah's smirk of satisfaction, nothing else.

An hour later, they heard a clamor in the front yard as a group from their old aerobics class arrived. Sarah set her brush aside. "You can finish up here if you like while I go downstairs and get everyone settled in."

Christine nodded. "Good idea. I have only half a wall to go, then I'll be down." When her friend left the room, Christine sighed in relief. She'd rather not be present when the group met Bear. She didn't want to endure the same speculation all over again. The others probably would not be as perceptive as Sarah, but she would rather keep painting than find out.

Besides, she was looking forward to seeing one room finished. She was eager for the satisfaction that came from witnessing a transformation.

When she was finished, she laid the roller in the pan and rose to survey her work. To shut out distractions and gain the full effect, she closed the door to the hallway and stood in the center of the room, hands on hips, turning in a slow circle.

She ran her gaze over the ceiling. Where there had been a web of cracks, there was now an unbroken expanse of white. Her eyes roamed the walls. Where there had been smelly layers of peeling wallpaper, there was now a smooth, pale glow of fresh color.

Her heart swelled with contentment. Someday the entire house would look just as clean and inviting as this room. It occurred to her that it had been a long time since she derived this much pleasure from her work. She felt more accomplishment from contributing to this transformation than from balancing schedules or pulling off a coup at the office. She was tempted to rationalize that, but at this moment it was enough to admit that she felt enormous fulfillment.

She heard a soft knock at the door. "Who is it?" she called.

"The major pain."

She felt her heart plummet to her feet at the wry sound of Bear's words. Surely, Sarah had not repeated what she'd said about him. No, Sarah wouldn't do that. It dawned on her that the empty house was like an echo chamber. Her voice, emphatic with emotion, had carried down the stairs to his curious ears.

Her face flushing, she opened the door and leaned against it for support as she glanced up at his face. "Well . . . of course, I was kidding."

"Of course." He stepped into the room, his gaze shifting to the freshly painted walls. A smile of genuine pleasure touched his lips. "I like it."

She joined him in the center of the room. "Doesn't it seem bigger now?"

"Yeah," he agreed.

Her creative tendency overrode her initial embarrassment. "Can you imagine a crib over there and white eyelet curtains on the window?"

His hands hooked on his waist as he nodded. "And white rugs," he added, glancing down, "which would look great after we refinish this hardwood floor."

"Yeah." She smiled up at him, and he felt his heart turn over in his chest. With her eyes warm with anticipation, her complexion bright with enthusiasm, he thought he'd never seen her look more beautiful. He had an overwhelming urge to kiss her. He was leaning toward her, and she was not moving away. His lips were hovering over hers when a shout of laughter broke loose downstairs. Startled they jumped apart, shifting guiltily, suddenly feeling awkward.

"Uh, I came up to get you because"—he had to think for an instant to remember his purpose—"because we're set to install the drywall in the great room."

"Oh, okay." Christine stooped to gather the paint supplies. "I'll just rinse these out in the kitchen first."

The rest of the day was spent with everyone hefting and toting, while Bear measured, cut, and positioned the drywall. The volunteers held it in place while he hammered it in. Everything was done according to his instructions. Installing drywall required Bear's experience and knowledge. The half-dozen volunteers worked well together, supplying the muscle necessary to carry and steady the heavy materials for long moments.

Late that afternoon, Tony Reyes and Bill Brosman ran out for pizza. When they returned, everyone fell upon the array of boxes.

"You know, Christine," began Bob Stansky, the young accountant stretched out on the floor, "one of the outfits I keep books for has an old delivery truck that I've depreciated out to the max. The owner is looking to trade it in for a new one." He swirled his soda around inside the can. "Sarah tells me you could use a truck on this job. I could suggest to the owner that he donate his old truck to your project instead of trading it."

"Really?" Christine's interest rang in her voice. "Oh, Bob, could we ever use a delivery truck!"

The young man nodded thoughtfully. "From an accounting standpoint, the owner would be better off to take the deduction for a charitable donation. I think he'd go for the idea."

"Super!" Christine exclaimed. "Is the truck in decent shape?"

"Sure. He just likes to replace them before they rack up a bunch of miles. An outfit services them and replaces the tires regularly. You'd be getting a good deal."

"I'll say," she said enthusiastically.

"Tell you what, I'll give you a call Monday and let you know what he wants to do one way or the other."

Christine tore off a scrap of paper and scribbled down her work number. "If I don't answer this extension, have them page me."

He pulled his wallet out of his hip pocket and slipped the paper inside. "The only catch is if he's game, you'll have to move on it right away. He's got this greedy brother-in-law who carts off every castoff he can get his hands on. Soon as he gets wind of this, he'll put in his bid."

"Hey, if it's go, we'll be over Monday afternoon to pick it up." She glanced at Bear. "Great news, huh?"

He looked sickly.

"Something wrong?" she asked.

"No, sounds great." He shook his head, and his hand moved to his stomach. "Must be the pepperoni."

Late the next afternoon, Christine scrambled up the steps. "Bear, where are you?" she called out, running through the house. "We're going to get the truck!" She found him in a bedroom upstairs, standing on a box, applying strips of fiberglass to patch the ceiling cracks. "Come on, Bear. We gotta strike while the iron's hot."

"I have to finish this," he said, without looking down. "Don't wait up. You go on."

"Bear, I need you to ride over there with me so you can drive the truck back here. Bob's staying late to meet us. He's got the paperwork all ready to go."

Dropping his arms to his sides, he shook the circulation back into them. He glanced at her, color flooding his face. "You don't need me. Bob will be there to help you."

She released an impatient breath. "You're missing the point, Bear. You ride with me over there. Then *you* drive the truck back, and I'll follow you in my car. Get it? It'll take two of us to pick it up."

He had a thoughtful look on his face as he stepped down from the box he was standing on. "I thought you said Bob would be there."

"I did."

"Well, there you are. Have him drive the truck over."

She shook her head in exasperation. "Then Bob doesn't have his car."

"Oh." Bear walked past her into the next room. She followed close on his heels. "I know I left my hammer somewhere."

Her eyes widened. "If I don't miss my guess, it's hanging on your tool belt where it always is." Bear was a fanatic about putting things back where they belonged.

He glanced at his hip absently. "Oh, sure enough. There it is."

"Bear, what's wrong?"

He shrugged. "I'm pretty busy here. I figure you can get anybody to just drive a truck over."

"Well, I could have someone else help me, but I should have already made arrangements by now. On such short notice, I might have trouble finding someone handy." A hurt look came into her eyes. "I just assumed you could take a few minutes to help me. After all, I've helped you a time or two."

He avoided making eye contact. "Have you cleared this with the mayor, about the truck and all? Are you sure we can accept it?"

"Of course. The mayor was delighted. The more stuff we get donated, the better. You know that."

He shrugged. "Well, a truck is a big-dollar item. I thought there might be restrictions on that . . . or something."

She wheeled around in front of him to block his path. "What is going on?" When she sensed that he might turn away, she grabbed the collar of his shirt. "You've always shot straight with me, Bear

Malone. You've shared your opinions even when I didn't want to hear them. So level with me now."

"It's not that I don't want to help you." She raised her brows to prompt him to continue. "It's just that . . . well, I don't know how to tell you this actually. . . ."

"Go on," she said. Though she knew that she couldn't stop him if he decided to walk away, her grip on his collar remained firm. "Just spit it out."

"I don't have a California driver's license."

"Oh." She released her hold on his collar. "Well, I'm driving on my Iowa license." She remembered that he'd said he'd lived in Colorado. "You have an out-of-state license, don't you?"

He shook his head.

"Well," she said thoughtfully, "it isn't wise to let your license expire. And while I don't advocate breaking the law, I don't think there would be a problem if you just drove the few miles it takes to bring the truck here. I'll take you down, and we can both apply for a California license tomorrow."

"I don't think so."

She arched her brow. "What now?"

There was a tortured look in his eyes, and his voice was low when he spoke. "I can't drive, okay?" He looked at her defiantly, his chin jutting out.

"Oh." A thought occurred to her. No wonder he was embarrassed. "I get it. You got your license revoked."

He shook his head.

"Suspended?"

He shook his head firmly. "What do you think I am, a criminal?"

"Well, why don't you tell me, so we can give up the twenty questions!"

He looked into her eyes, realizing that for the first time in his life he was more than inconvenienced, he was actually ashamed. "Since you must know, the truth is . . . I don't know how to drive."

"What?" she whispered. "Are you kidding?"

He glanced away, and she knew that he was serious.

"I'm sorry, Bear. I had no idea."

"Well, now you know."

She closed her hand over his. "Do you have some phobia about driving. Is that it?"

"No, that isn't it." Now he looked exasperated. "When I turned sixteen, I was in boarding school. I had no car. No one did. There were no drivers' ed classes. So I figured I'd learn after I got into college. Turns out, I was used to public transportation by then. I got involved in environmental causes and didn't want to add to the pollution, so . . . I never learned to drive."

"Don't you wish you could?"

"Actually, until a few moments ago, I was pretty content the way I was. But now, yeah, I wish I could drive. I wish I could go get the truck with you. I wish I could pick up supplies and donations sometimes." He looked wistful.

She nodded. "Well, hey, I could teach you to drive."

"Well, maybe. But that won't help you today."

She shrugged. "Perhaps someone there can drive it out. Or I guess I could call Percy."

With that last suggestion, Bear's eyes glazed over. It was humiliating enough to tell Christine that he couldn't drive, but for that jerk to find out and lord it over him. He wasn't sure he could handle that. "We don't have a phone here," he said. "Remember?"

"Right."

She drove over alone, determined at least to get the paperwork signed. That way the truck would be safely assigned to the project before the owner could change his mind.

Bob was kind enough to drive the truck to the house, and she drove him back in her car to pick up his vehicle.

Bear had remained inside the house throughout the comings and goings, but when she returned to the house for the last time she found him in the driver's seat of the truck cab, gazing at the gizmos on the dashboard.

She stepped up on the running board and looked at him. "Well, what do you think? It belongs to the renewal project now—signed, sealed, and delivered."

"It's nice." His tone was noncommittal.

"It's a manual five-speed," she said.

"I know." He eyed the tall stick shift warily.

She shrugged. "It's easier to learn on an automatic, but you ought to know how to drive a manual transmission as well."

He nodded, but not too convincingly.

"My car is a manual five-speed. It's very responsive and easy to shift. I think you'd have a much easier time learning to drive a car before you progress to the truck."

"That makes sense."

Her eyes widened. It was a novel experience for them to agree on something. She took it as a good omen.

"Well," she said, "when do you want to get started?"

"What?" he asked as if he'd actually just heard her voice for the first time.

"We could have your first driving lesson this evening."

He glanced at the sky. "It's almost sundown. I think we should wait for broad daylight."

"We have an hour till sunset. Besides, with my work schedule, I won't have a day free until Saturday and we'll be busy with the house. No time like the present."

He looked at her. Why did she have to be so damned efficient? Why couldn't she put off a few things, like everybody else? He needed a little time to think this over, get himself psyched up for it. "What's the rush?" he asked.

"No rush, actually. I just thought the sooner you got your license, the sooner you could pick up supplies when they're offered to us. In a few weeks they'll be renovating an old building downtown. I understand that they're letting people have priceless materials like broken marble, tin ceiling tiles, just for hauling them off." She shrugged. "I'll be tied up at work, so I guess we'll just miss out on that one."

He knew that she was pushing his buttons now. He'd read the news, too, and he hated for them to miss out on the interesting materials they could pick up for the house.

"We could get started now," he said finally without much enthusiasm, "except I don't have a learner's permit." Ah, he thought gratefully, saved by a technicality.

She shrugged. "No problem. We won't have you driving on public streets. There's a perfectly good alternative."

Seven

"A *cemetery?* Ah, come on, Christine!" Pure shock registered on his face as she drove through the open iron gates onto hallowed grounds. "You can't expect me to concentrate on a driving lesson in a *cemetery* for heaven's sake!"

"Why not? Think about it. Where could you be safer? There's practically no traffic. Why, I don't even see another car. It's quiet and private. No cops, no traffic lights—it's perfect."

"What about the headstones?" The place was *full* of them.

She chuckled. "No problem. You're going to stay on the paved lane that winds through." She patted his shoulder soothingly. "Look, I've come here a few times just to think. Believe me, in a place like this, you can get your priorities straight in no time at all."

She switched off the key and got out of her car. With quick steps, she circled her car to open his door. "Hop out now. We're changing seats."

He sat there for a moment, looking up at her. "I

don't know about this. Somehow it just doesn't seem right."

"I don't think anybody here is going to mind."

He climbed out slowly. Reluctantly, he walked around the front of the car, taking care not to read any of the names on the markers. As much as possible, he didn't want to intrude on anyone.

Once he'd settled behind the wheel, he tried to focus on the gauges, dials, buttons, and knobs. "Looks like the cockpit of a seven forty-seven," he mumbled. He pulled the shoulder harness across his body and listened to the solid click as he fastened it.

Christine gave him time to look, touch, and get acquainted. Suddenly, his head snapped around, and he looked into her eyes earnestly. "I think I know how much this car means to you."

She shrugged. "I like it."

The furrow between his brows deepened. "It's valuable, and it means a lot to you."

"Well, the bottom line is," she began in a confidential tone, "I'm still making payments on it."

He shook his head. "I say we rent a car for driving lessons. Better yet, let's find a simulator."

"I appreciate your considerate attitude, but let's face it, Malone, you're stalling."

His jaw tensed. He'd been afraid it would come to this. She wasn't going to imply that he was chicken and get away with it. "Right," he said in a tight voice.

"Okay," she said, her voice calm and reassuring. "Let's take it slow and easy."

He swallowed thickly and gripped the wheel. Next to an abscessed tooth, this was going to be his favorite thing.

She took him through the basic H pattern of the

gear shift lever and acquainted him with the clutch, accelerator, and brake pedals. To avoid confusion, she tried to show him only the controls he would need for his lesson today.

He pressed in the clutch, feeling clumsy, as though his feet were too large for the pedals. With a twist of the key, the motor sprang to life. He took hold of the gear shift lever. She closed her hand lightly over his, guiding him gently into first gear.

"Now let out on the clutch as you press down the accelerator." Her voice was low and gentle. "Easy, easy."

The car started forward slowly. His attention was diverted to the tree-shaded lane coming up ahead, and he forgot about his feet. When he popped the clutch, the car lunged. Instinctively, he slammed on the brake, nearly standing the little red BMW on its nose. The tires squealed as the engine promptly died.

Christine winced, but her voice remained calm. "It's okay. Turn off the key and take a moment to relax before we try again."

He waited till his heart rate returned to something close to normal. "All right." He took a deep breath. "I'm ready." He restarted the engine and waited until it was purring rhythmically. He eased in the clutch and shifted to first. His jaw firmed resolutely as he stared through the windshield and slowly let out on the clutch and gently pressed down the accelerator.

For an instant, nothing happened. Christine's hands balled into tight fists on her lap. The car was straining at the bit.

"Give it more gas," she said quietly. He was being so cautious with the clutch that he was barely pressing the accelerator. She slowly reached across and lightly tapped his right knee. "Press down easy."

As he did so, the car moved forward. "See," she said encouragingly, "we're moving right along."

He glanced at the speedometer. "Well, we're going all of seventeen miles an hour."

The engine was whining as she suggested. "Better shift to second."

He glanced at her, his eyes round, his mind blank.

She nodded. She recognized panic when she saw it. "Press in the clutch." She guided his hand on the stick shift drawing it back into second. "Now ease out on the clutch." The car lurched once. "Not so fast," she warned. "Slow and easy. More accelerator. That's good."

As their speed increased, his adrenaline was pumping. "The road," he began in a strained voice, "is a T ahead." He was staring wide-eyed at the end of the road as though it was the end of the world.

"Yes," she said firmly, "you'll have to turn."

"Which way?" He was trying to keep the panic out of his voice, but all he could see straight ahead was a huge stone mausoleum.

"Your choice," she said in a choked whisper.

He waited too long to make a decision. Christine gasped as they continued through the T, heading straight for the unrelenting wall of gray stone. "Turn," she cried.

He cranked the wheel to the right, and the car spun around in a tight arc. A black wheel slipped off the lane onto the soft grass. Bear overcorrected and whipped the wheel hard to the right again. His shoulder slammed against the window as the car crossed the lane headed for a tall marker with the inscription *Rest In Peace.*

Christine reached out to brace herself against the center console. "Turn the wheel back," she said, "easy." The right front and rear wheels slipped off the lane onto the shoulder. In an attack of panic, Bear's right hand left the shift lever to cross himself quickly. "Forgive me, Father . . ."

Christine's left hand shot out to steady the wheel. In a split second, they were careening through the long shadows down the middle of the lane.

"See," she said, "she's very responsive, so you just handle her gently." She kept her hand on the wheel to guide him through the feel of the curves until his confidence grew. Then she slipped her hand back on her lap.

They practiced stops and starts until the car took off with only a lurch now and then. Several times her right foot slammed the floorboard to no avail. Consciously, she knew that she couldn't stop the car, but still her instincts took over occasionally.

As he learned how to use the pedals and turn the wheel simultaneously, she taught him to add the signal blinkers.

His nerves began to subside, and she got him up to third gear, guiding the shifter through the H pattern. He got heavy-footed on the accelerator and laid a strip of rubber down the lane, the back end fishtailing several feet before he brought the car to an abrupt stop.

He looked at her apologetically. "Sorry."

She chuckled softly. "Bet that doesn't happen around here too often."

He grinned back at her. "It's getting dark. Maybe

you better take over." He switched off the motor, and threw open their doors. As Bear stepped out, he sent up a silent apology for any disrespect his disasters might have caused.

They met in front of the hood. As Christine started past him, Bear reached out and grasped her shoulders. "Hey," he began softly, "from one hardhead to another, thanks."

Her lip curved in a smile. "You're okay, Malone." He was more than okay, but she didn't tell him that.

He smiled into her eyes. "I'm grateful for the lesson. You made me want something I didn't even know I was missing. It's better to know how."

She nodded, touched by his sincerity. He wasn't given to smooth lines and easy come-ons. She was beginning to appreciate the fact that he was masculine without acting macho, confident without acting cocky. "Well, I have to admit it's an afternoon I won't forget." They both chuckled, and he stared into her eyes for a moment. Then before the moment passed, he brought his head down and kissed her once. It was a warm, affectionate kiss that flooded her heart with a delicious glow.

He released her shoulders and stepped around her on his way to the passenger seat. She paused to catch her breath before continuing on toward the driver's seat. He'd taken her by surprise, but he hadn't taken advantage of her. She could have drawn back, but she hadn't wanted to.

She drove him home in companionable silence, realizing that she couldn't blame her response to his kiss last Friday night on the beer or the moonlight. Perhaps Sarah had been right when she'd said that she sensed a strong magnetism between them. There was certainly something between them. Now she had to figure out what it was and what to do about it.

She left him off at the restaurant beside the sandy road that led to his house. He offered to buy her dinner, but she begged off, following her instinct to draw back and let things sort themselves out in her head.

The next Saturday, Bear was the only one present when she showed up early to work at the house. They greeted each other and went about their work in separate areas. She went upstairs to paint, while he smoothed thin layers of plaster on the new drywall in the great room.

Hours later, he stood at the foot of the stairs, calling up to her, "Hey, Christine, you have a visitor waiting down here."

"Coming," she called. Who could it be? If it was Sarah Chetter, Tony Reyes, Bob Stansky, or Bill Brosman or any of the other helpers, Bear wouldn't be calling her down. She stuck her paintbrush in a can of water and tapped the lid back on the paint can. She shrugged as she wiped her hands and headed for the stairs.

When she got downstairs, the house looked empty. "Hello?" she called.

"Hello yourself, stranger," Percy said as he strolled into the room from the kitchen.

Christine looked at him curiously. "I didn't expect to find you here."

He stood in the middle of the great room, his hands shoved deep into the pockets of his pleated pants. His tie hung loose in the crisp collar of his button-down shirt. The gold insignia on his navy blazer glinted in the muted sunlight filtering through the windows in long shafts.

As always, his shoes were those perfectly polished, cordovan Gucci loafers. She found herself wondering how it was that they always looked brand-new, not even a crease to show that they were broken in. Perhaps he had scads of them. She never saw him when he wasn't wearing them. Signature shoes—how like him they were.

She watched with interest as he walked toward her, placing his heels flat on the floor, carefully avoiding contact with the boxes of supplies scattered about, moving his feet in a shuffling pattern. That was how he did it, she decided. He placed his feet so carefully, so strategically, that the only part of the shoes that received any wear at all were the soles.

"You look happy to see me," he announced.

It was then that Christine realized that she was smiling. She didn't bother to tell him that it was discovering the secret of his shoes rather than his company that made her smile. "Of course."

"Haven't seen you lately," he said, shuffling to the front windows.

"I'm at work a good deal of the time." She slid down to sit on the bottom step.

"Or here."

She shrugged. "I'm not that hard to find."

"Oh no? You're never in your office."

She nodded. "I can get more done moving around the plant."

"I hate to go out into the plant." He tapped his toe silently. "Too dirty."

"If you think it's dirty there, I shudder to imagine what you think of this place." She wondered why he'd come, but decided to let him tell her in his own good time.

He tossed her a look over his shoulder. "Don't ask." He shook his head. "I thought you would have gotten this out of your system by now."

"Gotten what out of my system?"

"This do-gooder gig you're on."

She found herself growing impatient waiting to find out what he wanted. "Exactly why are you here, Percy?"

A long moment passed while Percy frowned, looking out the front window. "Did you know that," he said slowly, "that big guy is out there backing that delivery van to the end of the driveway and driving it back up . . . over and over again?"

"Yes."

The look on Percy's face was incredulous. "What is the deal? Doesn't he know how to drive?"

"He's learning."

"Ha," Percy said harshly, "he's a bigger dummy than I thought."

"He is not a dummy," Christine said in a tight voice.

"Well, there's no accounting for taste, is there?"

"At least, his taste is not a matter of accounting."

"What do you mean by that?"

Christine cocked her head and looked at Percy, wondering how it was that she had ever put up with him. "Just that you play all the angles, Percy. Anything to get ahead."

"Just good business." He turned to face her. "You should know that better than anyone. How else would you be the fastest corporate rocket at ElectroFirst?"

"Is that what you think I am?"

He bowed from the waist. "Who else has leap-frogged through promotions in such a short time?"

"Jealous?"

"Admiring." He turned on one of those mega-watt smiles. "I figure a body could learn a lot of shortcuts from you."

"You might try hard work . . . long hours."

"Yeah, right." He looked irritated. "I can see you're not going to share any real secrets with me today."

"Those are the real secrets."

His face flushed. "I won't take up any more of your valuable time here"—he glanced out the window at the sound of grinding gears—"building with bozo. So let's cut to the bottom line. The company party is next weekend. I think it would be great if we went together, don't you?"

"Let me see if I've got this right. You want me to go to the company party with you so you can show up with someone you think will further your career."

He opened his mouth in a look of mock outrage. "Hey, I don't think you'd lose any points with old man Montgomery if you showed up with me either. Politics, baby. Like it or not, you know it works."

"I don't like it."

Percy's lip curled as he bobbed his head up and down. "And I guess you'd rather show up with bozo, huh? In his delivery van? Driving with his learner's permit, huh?"

She leaned forward, hugging her knees. "You got that right."

He rocked back on his heels, his expression deadpan. "You're not serious."

"Maybe I am." Until that moment, she'd given

the party little thought. It hadn't mattered to her whether she showed up with an escort or not. One thing she knew for certain, she would not go with Percy Dupres.

He shook his head in disbelief. "If you go to the party with him"—he jerked a thumb in the direction of the driveway—"you will be the laughing-stock of the entire company. I hope you know that."

She shrugged. "We'll see."

He strode to the front door and jerked it open. He paused just long enough to glare over his shoulder at her. "Get a life," he said angrily and charged out the door.

She followed him out on the newly floored front porch and watched him trudge across the beaten down, dusty yard. For a moment, she envisioned herself in the uniform of a major league manager kicking dust onto his Gucci loafers. The thought brought a smile to her lips. When Percy glanced over his shoulder, the expression on her face seemed to enrage him.

Bear was climbing out of the truck when Percy paused ten feet from him to say, "Well, I certainly hope you fit in at the party."

Bear lifted a brow and regarded Percy as he would a pesky gnat. "What party?"

Percy let out an exasperated sigh as if he were out of patience speaking with fools. "Your little date to the company party with Christine," he snapped.

Bear wasn't sure what was going on, but he knew he didn't like the tone of Percy's voice or his attitude. Bear lowered his head and took a step toward him. Percy made a dash for his Ferrari, unconcerned for the moment that crunching through the gravel was leaving white chalky marks on his shoes. The Ferrari spun out of the driveway and roared down the street.

Bear looked at Christine curiously as he climbed onto the porch. "What's he babbling about?"

She smiled. "I told him that I was asking you to accompany me to the company party next weekend."

The look on his face revealed he had reservations. "You sure you want to do that?"

"Yes." It was the simple truth. There was no one else she'd rather be with than Bear Malone, though she hadn't admitted it to anyone, including herself.

"You know, as far as I'm concerned, I think we should put that silly challenge between us to rest." He hooked his hands on his waist and faced her squarely. "I don't happen to think we've proved anything . . . except that probably both of us are guilty of jumping to some conclusions. So let's not ask each other to go anywhere to prove some point to ourselves or to anybody else, okay?"

She looked into his eyes, into the straightforward honesty in those deep blue depths. "Agreed."

He nodded and started around her to the front door. "Bear?" He stopped, shoulder to shoulder, beside her. "As one friend to another, I'd like to ask you to go to the party with me. I can't promise that it'll be a good time, but we can duck out early if it's a drag."

The corners of his mouth lifted, and his eyes smiled into hers. "What time?"

The following Saturday evening, Christine parked her car on the street outside the lavish blufftop condominium owned by her boss and chosen by him as the site for his annual company bash. Bear hopped out on the passenger side and walked around to open her door for her. She stepped out, locked the door, and slipped the key into her black leather evening bag.

Bear threaded her arm through his and let his gaze sweep over her. Her off-the-shoulder dress was elegant in its simplicity, revealing her creamy shoulders and outlining her shapely figure. "You look fantastic."

She smiled up at him as they started down the sidewalk. "I could say the same about you." He wore his dark double-breasted suit with a casual grace.

Couples were gathering at the corner, and on the sidewalk across the street. Christine noted that while Bear's looks might not have been as slick as those of the executives at ElectroFirst, they were far more compelling. He drew admiring glances from the ladies they passed, glances that returned to linger.

They made a handsome couple striding up the walkway, his powerful, broad-shouldered build contrasting with her rounded, feminine shape.

"Welcome, Christine." R. C. Montgomery, standing at his open front door, gathered her hand in his and patted it affectionately. "I'm so glad you could make it."

"Thank you, Mr. Montgomery."

"R.C.," he said emphatically. "You must call me R.C. I'm not going to remind you again." He was a tall, distinguished-looking man in his late fifties who stood ramrod straight and whose dark eyes looked at her with piercing directness.

"R.C.," she repeated dutifully, "I'd like to introduce Bear Malone."

The two men shook hands, looking into each other's eyes and taking each other's measure in a brief moment. "Glad to meet you, Mr. Malone. Come right in."

R.C. made a sweeping gesture with his right arm, and they walked past him into the two-story foyer. A uniformed maid accepted the black cashmere coat Christine was carrying over her arm and ushered them into a huge living room with a long wall of floor-to-ceiling windows that looked out over the Pacific.

The room was crowded, and Christine recognized familiar faces from ElectroFirst and its associates. Bear accepted two flutes of champagne from a waiter and handed one to Christine. She greeted passing people, including Bear in the conversations.

They made their way to the windows where they stood for a moment, transfixed by the view. "My favorite hour," she told him. They watched the final long rays of the setting sun upon the vast water with a quiet reverence while around them conversations bubbled.

"Bear Malone? Is that you?"

They turned to face a youthful-looking man with an engaging grin. Bear scrutinized the man for an instant.

"Give you a hint," the man said. "We took several undergraduate art classes together."

A light came into Bear's eyes. "Jake Mackey?"

"That's me!" The man looked enormously pleased that Bear recognized him. "Hold on. I want my wife to meet you. Honey, come over here," he said to a tall brunette nearby. "Honey, this is Bear

Malone. Remember me telling you about him? One of the best tackles UCLA ever had."

The woman extended her hand. "Janis Mackey."

Bear shook her hand and introduced Christine.

"Man, I looked at the windows and saw these wide shoulders blocking out the sun, and bam, it hit me, that's gotta be Bear Malone. How ya doin', big guy?"

"Fine and you?"

"Great. I got this job in advertising, so Janis and I moved up here with the kids. We do the Electro-First account, so Montgomery sent us an invite. You still into wood carving and all?"

Bear nodded. "To a degree."

Jake threw his arm around his wife's shoulders. "You oughta see this guy work. He sculpts his wood carvings with a chain saw!"

"Really?" Janis said with a smile.

Christine looked up at Bear. "You do?"

The corners of Bear's eyes crinkled as he looked down at the surprise on her face. "Remind me to show you my etchings sometime."

"I will," she said.

"So tell me, do you work for ElectroFirst?" Jake asked, looking at Bear.

He shook his head. "No, but Christine does."

"I heard you went into the pros after college," Jake said.

Bear nodded. "Played for the Broncos for a little while till I messed up my knees."

Christine's eyes widened. He'd never told her about his college days or what he did afterward. She should have guessed he'd played football, but for the Broncos? It amazed her to discover she didn't know much about this man.

"Well, what are you doing these days?" Jake asked.

Bear looked at him. "Something I'm really excited about."

"Yeah?"

"Christine and I are involved in a volunteer project in Santa Cruz to convert run-down houses into affordable homes for familes."

"Really?" Jake and Janis exchanged a look of interest. "Do you have to have skills to get into this?"

Bear looked at Christine. "Talk to the recruiter here."

Christine smiled at them. "We're looking for anyone who could donate time and effort to help with the physical work or solicit donations. No skills required."

"We would be interested in helping out," Janis said. "How do we get in touch with you?"

"You can call me at home or leave a message at ElectroFirst." She produced a card from her evening bag and handed it to Janis.

"Super," Jake said. He glanced at his watch with a frown. "Hey, I hate to go, but we live in San Jose and we're breaking in a new baby-sitter, so we better head over the hill." He nodded at Christine. "You'll be hearing from one of us."

"Great," she said.

Across the room, she saw Percy in deep conversation with Montgomery. She thought she saw him gesturing once in her direction, but she couldn't be sure. On the other side of Percy stood his tall, blond secretary, looking alone and neglected. Christine sympathized with the girl. She knew how inattentive Percy could be at functions like this.

She looked up at Bear. "You didn't tell me you

went to UCLA or that you played for the Broncos."

He shrugged. "I told you I moved around a lot."

"But you didn't say why."

He shrugged.

"You're not one to brag, are you?"

"No," he replied simply. "It's important to live in the present. What I'm proud of is the work we're doing through the project."

"Me too." She liked the sound of that, and she especially appreciated the way he now always included her by referring to the project in terms of *we* rather than *I*, even though he was the only full-time worker.

"You know," she said, tilting her head to one side and looking up at him, "I don't imagine these hors d'oeuvres are going to hold you for long." She glanced down at a tray of intricate, dainty appetizers.

"No?"

"Remember I've seen you down an entire pizza for a midafternoon snack."

"You have a point. So what are you suggesting?"

She leaned toward him and lowered her voice to a confidential tone. "That we blow this place and get some real food."

"I'm right behind you."

They threaded their way through the room, looking for their host but he was nowhere to be seen. In the foyer, the maid handed Christine her coat. Bear took it from her and was slipping it over her shoulders when Montgomery appeared. "Leaving so soon?"

Christine looked up at him. "Thank you, R.C. We've have a lovely time, but we have another engagement."

There was a slight pause before R.C. replied, "I

understand, my dear. I'm glad that you could come. It was good to meet you, Mr. Malone."

Bear nodded. "My pleasure, Mr. Montgomery."

Outside, Christine took a deep breath of ocean breeze. Montgomery had said the right things, but she'd sensed an undercurrent. She pushed it from her mind. Montgomery was the kind of boss who made his opinions known. If there was a problem, she'd know about it soon enough. For now, she had the rest of the evening to herself and Bear Malone, a prospect she wanted to enjoy without the intrusion of nagging worries.

They found themselves striding down the sidewalk arm in arm with the enthusiasm of youngsters who've just found out that their afternoon classes were canceled.

"Where do you want to go?" she asked when she'd settled behind the wheel.

"Home, James," he said with a deep chuckle.

"Right on." She fired the engine and headed in that general direction. They could pick a destination later, far from the shadow of Montgomery's condo. It pleased her that Bear could joke about her chauffeuring him.

"You won't always be the designated driver, you know."

"No?"

"I'm going to take my driver's test in a few weeks."

"Then we'd better wedge in a couple more lessons."

"Bill Brosman came by work a couple days last week, and we practiced driving an hour here and there."

"Great," she said with a smile.

"I have you to thank for getting me started."

"Oh, don't thank me," she said with a shrug. "You could have learned whenever you wanted."

"For some reason, I was content with public transportation and bumming rides until I met you."

"And I came along to lead you down the paths of temptation and materialism," she joked.

"You had the right idea. I should know how to drive a car. I guess I've always had buddies who wanted to drive, so I put it off. But especially in case of an emergency, it's something I ought to be able to do competently."

"And legally," she added, and he chuckled.

When she pulled into the familiar parking lot of the little restaurant, she turned to him. "You'll have to tell me where you'd like to have dinner," she said.

He glanced at the illuminated digital clock on the dash. It was past nine o'clock. "I've got a suggestion," he said. "You could drive on down the lane to my place, and I'll whip up some Chicken Malone for us."

"You don't think I'll get stuck in the sand?"

He shook his head. "The roadbed is solid enough." He looked at her apologetically. "I didn't want you to drive down there before because . . . well, I thought you might get bent out of shape if you got your car dirty. That was before I knew you better."

She nodded. "Back when you thought I was a yuppie?"

He grinned sheepishly in the muted glow from the dashboard. "Yeah, back then."

"I guess we're both guilty of judging from appearances." Gradually, things between them had changed. Walls had crumbled. "Perhaps we should start over. Deal?"

"Deal." He smiled at her, marveling at how much his feelings for her had changed. Her open mind impressed him, along with her sense of fair play. Somewhere along the line, his opinion had modified from outright disapproval to grudging respect to admiration.

"Chicken Malone, huh?" She pretended to be carefully weighing all of her options.

"Award-winning recipe," he said in a deep, tantalizing voice.

"Don't tell me that in your secret past you've been a world-famous chef too?"

"Not me, that's in my sister's past, but she taught me how to prepare her secret recipe."

"This I gotta try."

"This, you will."

Eight

Christine drove down the narrow lane to Bear's beach house and parked in the one-car garage attached to a small outbuilding. "What's this?" she asked him, peering at the sign on the door.

"It's a studio workshop."

She peered at the sign and read it aloud, "Open When I Am Here." She glanced at him curiously. "Is that how you run a business?"

He shrugged. "This was my mother's home. She ran a little art shop out of her studio, mostly for her friends who walked the beach. They had a running joke about her hours. If they dropped in and she was there, she was open for business. If she wasn't, then the place was locked up tight and she called it closed." A wistful sadness crossed his face.

"Sounds like she had a delightful personality," she said quietly.

He looked at her in the dim light. "She did." It occurred to him that his mother would have liked Christine. She would have admired her spirit, her fire, and her kindness.

He turned, and she followed him up the steps. He unlocked the door, reached in to flip on the lights, and swung the door open for her.

She stepped inside and looked around. The home was small, simple, and neat, but it seemed as though it was designed on a grander scale with its vaulted ceilings and tall windows that looked out on the surf. She toured the first floor. There were artistic touches everywhere. Even the furniture in the living and dining areas was handmade.

"You carved this with a . . . chain saw?" she asked, running her fingers over the rough-hewn tabletop.

He nodded slowly, looking almost chagrined. "My mother insisted on having it here."

She ran her hands over the smoothed, hollowed-out trunks of trees that formed the backs of the chairs. They had a solid, warm feeling, like the man who had made them. She looked up at him. "Built to last," she said.

He nodded. Built to last was the phrase he thought of the first time he saw her figure sway through the front door of the house they were rebuilding. Now that he knew her better, he knew the words fit perfectly.

He showed her the small guest room downstairs and the loft upstairs where he slept and looked out from a balcony to the sea. They stepped through the double door out onto the balcony. "It's so beautiful here," she said.

"It's rather private, actually. People walk the beach here, but they don't disturb the residents."

"I'd love to walk out there," she said.

"Then after our supper, we'll take a walk."

She looked down at her holiday dress. "It seems that I'm never dressed for it."

"While I fix dinner, you can change if you'd like. I'm certainly not going to cook in these duds. I'm messy in the kitchen."

"Do you have something to fit me?" It was a sure bet that they couldn't share jeans.

"My sister left some beach clothes in the guest room closet, and she's about your size. Help yourself."

"You don't mind?"

"Not at all, though I must admit I've been enjoying the view all evening." He glanced at her creamy shoulders and the interesting way the dress draped across her bodice. He might be less tempted to touch if she were wearing something less enticing.

"Thanks." She actually blushed, and it occurred to him once again that she wasn't as worldly as she seemed. At the foot of the stairs, she headed for the guest room and he headed for the kitchen.

In the closet, she found a pair of baggy jeans and an oversize shirt that would do. She found a pair of socks in a drawer and tennis shoes on the floor of the closet that were only slightly too large.

When she wandered into the kitchen, he was standing with his back to her, wearing jeans, a T-shirt, and wrapped in a huge chef's apron. "Mmmm, smells good," she said, moving to his side. She watched him add a mixture of white wine, lemon juice, and sour cream to chicken breasts simmering in a skillet.

"You must swear never to reveal what you've just watched me do."

"The secret, huh?"

He grinned at her. "Not really. The recipe, more or less, was published in a magazine in that rack over there. Would you care for a glass of wine?"

"Yes, thanks." Christine picked up the magazine and flipped through it. "Hey, I think I found it." She joined him as he poured her a glass of wine from the bottle he used to pour wine into the skillet.

He handed her a long-stemmed glass. She took a sip. "This is good stuff."

"My sister says if it's good enough to drink, then it's good enough to cook with."

"I see that you don't use exact measurements."

He nodded. "Neither does my sister. It never turns out quite the same way twice."

"I imagine that keeps things interesting."

"You got it." He returned to the stove to check under a pot lid.

She held up a page with a picture of a smiling couple. "Is this your sister?"

He nodded. "That's Annie and her husband, Taylor."

"Handsome couple." Christine replaced the magazine and carried her wineglass to look at the collection of photographs on the wall behind the table. "This must be them in this picture."

Bear turned and looked over his shoulder. "That's them with Brian, the boy they adopted. They're in the process of adopting two more kids."

"They sound like wonderful people."

"You'll have to meet them next time they visit. I think you'd enjoy them, and I know they'd like you."

She wandered back to his side where he was preparing a salad. "Let me help you with that."

He shook his head. "You can wait on me when I come to your house."

"My apartment," she corrected. "And believe me, it isn't as homey and inviting as it is here."

"You don't take much time out for yourself, do you?"

She shook her head. "Always too busy."

"Maybe you should." She looked happier here than she did at Montgomery's party.

"Maybe I will one of these days."

"Well, that's a start." He carried steaming platters to the table. "Time to eat."

They clinked their glasses and drank a toast to the success of the project they both loved. Christine held up her hand to object when he served her generous portions. Then she tasted his cooking.

"This is superb. No wonder your sister won a contest with this recipe. I love it."

"I'll tell her you liked it."

She wondered if he meant that, if they'd even see each other after the house was finished. They had seemed like such opposites, and they were both still stubborn in their ways. There was much about his past that she didn't know, more than she'd ever imagined.

"You know," she began, "with your art degree, I'm surprised you aren't working in a museum or in advertising like your friend Jake."

"I tried the commercial art field, but it didn't seem satisfying to me."

"A lot of people don't find their nine-to-five jobs all that satisfying, but they do help pay the bills."

He shrugged. "It seems to me that we have only a short time on this earth. It's important to me to do something that I feel is worthwhile."

"Not everyone can afford that luxury."

He looked at her for a moment. "Please don't take this the wrong way, but I don't consider that a luxury. For me, it's a necessity that I've come to require over the years."

She set her wineglass aside. "You can tell me that it's none of my business, but I'm curious how you can do volunteer work and afford this place too."

"I have investments. Some of them from my mother's estate, some of them I made when I was making a big salary. I'm no longer interested in running the rat race for riches and status. My needs are few, actually."

"Not everyone has that option."

"I wish everyone did. If I decided to take a job for hire, it will have to be something I believe is worthwhile. At the same time, I don't hunger for a lot of things."

"Neither do I, actually."

His brows lifted with curiosity, but he remained silent. The moments stretched by, inviting her to elaborate.

She released the long breath that she was holding. "I wonder if you still think that's what I'm all about."

His gaze was penetrating. "You tell me."

She wondered what to say, where to start. "I wanted to accomplish more than just keeping house for someone who'd never appreciate it. I went to college on scholarships and worked hard to maintain them, but they didn't cover all my expenses, so I took out college loans. I'm still paying them back, along with car payments, living expenses, et cetera. I'd like nothing better than to just work on the project like you do."

His brows lifted at that. "Would you? I'd think anyone who's been as successful as you have in the workplace would miss it."

She sighed. "I honestly don't know. I guess I'm one of those women who want it all."

"That has come to mean a husband and children too."

She shrugged. "I don't know about that either. I do know that I want to be a person in my own right, not just an extension of someone else."

"Like your mother?"

He had a good memory, and he was perceptive too. "Yes, like her."

"Did she tell you she was unhappy with her life?" he asked casually as he sliced his chicken.

Christine frowned at her plate. "She wouldn't do that, but I don't see how she could be."

When he looked up, his eyes probed hers. "Perhaps you ought to ask her sometime."

Christine's chin jutted out. "Maybe I will."

They chatted as they finished their meal and stacked the dishes. He looked at her and asked, "Ready for dessert?"

"After that meal? No way."

"A walk on the beach?"

She nodded enthusiastically.

"On one condition," he told her.

"What?"

He chuckled deep and full. "We stay dry this time."

"You've got a deal."

He gave her one of his jackets to slip into and she giggled over the way it hung down to her knees. "It'll keep you warm," he said with a wide grin as he pulled on a hooded sweatshirt. He threw his arm around her shoulders, and they started off down the beach.

The night was shrouded in fog. The surf was only a few feet away. They could feel its pulse through their shoes; they could hear it slap the sand, but they couldn't see it through the gauzy mist. It seemed they were the only two people walking the beach, alone and far from the rest of the world.

They walked a long time without talking, lost in their own thoughts. When they turned to head back, they moved slower as if reluctant to let the evening end. After a while, Bear stopped. "We're here."

She looked around. They were caught in a bank of fog. "How can you tell?" She turned to face him.

"The house is directly east of here. Trust me."

"I trust you," she said simply, looking up into his eyes. They were standing close, facing each other, his arm still slung over her shoulders.

His dark gaze dropped to her mouth, and the look in his gaze was intimate . . . tactile. "I wonder," he said softly, "what would happen if I . . ." He lowered his head to hers to nuzzle, to smell the sweetness of her skin and the softness of her face next to his. He offered a tenderness he hadn't known was his to give.

She stepped into his embrace, seeking the warmth, the intimacy. If he had demanded more of her, she could have rebelled, but his gentleness was her undoing.

When she strained closer, his mouth swooped down to take hers, and her eyelids fluttered closed. Sensations swirled through her like the tendrils of mist floating around them.

She'd been drawn to him for weeks, but had also been disturbed by her feelings. It had frightened her how much she'd missed him the few times she'd arrived at the house to find him not there. Somewhere along the line, he'd come to mean a great deal to her. She'd fought that; she'd fought him along with her feelings for him.

She didn't want to want him like this, yet it seemed futile to resist. She believed herself too practical for fantasies, but had discovered that no one was that practical. She'd argued with herself endlessly that her feelings for him were illogical, but so were attractions, and this one had become undeniable.

She strained closer, wrapping her arms around him. They'd spent countless hours together, resisting needs that they'd awakened in each other until their desire had become impossible to ignore.

She whispered his name on a helpless moan, in a cry of surrender. Her voice threw him. In that instant, he suspected how much it cost her to give in to longings she'd denied for so long. His mouth moved over hers hungrily in what became a hot, frantic kiss.

Only he could ignite a desire so desperate. Her hands raced up his back, plunging into his hair, drawing his head down. She wanted the kiss to never end.

She was driving him crazy. He'd thought he could resist her if he dared her, challenged her, criticized her, competed with her. None of it had worked as he'd planned. It had all backfired. He wanted her as he'd never wanted anyone in his life.

He deepened the kiss, lingering over it, savoring it. So many times he had wanted to do this, to release the restraints and take her face in his hands and make love to that mouth that taunted and seduced him in his dreams.

He knew that she wanted him desperately, just as much as he wanted her. He was tempted to drag her to the house or take her right here, quickly before she could change her mind. But he needed more from her than that. He needed to have her consciously give herself to him. He didn't want to wake to face accusations in her eyes, guilt in his own. Whatever they did or did not do together tonight would have to be mutually decided, mutually shared.

With a groan, he pulled his lips from hers. His gaze raked over her flushed features, her half-closed eyelids. "Is this what you want too?" he asked her on a ragged breath.

She nodded slowly, tensing her fingers, clutching his shoulders.

"I need to hear it."

She swallowed around the lump that sprang into her throat. "I . . . need you, Bear. I want you." She'd deal with the consequences of those feelings later.

His hand closed over hers, and they trudged across the sand to the house. Silently, they entered the dark living room, then he led her upstairs to his loft where he clicked on a small bedside lamp.

He turned to face her, his eyes dark with need. Her gaze locked with his as she dropped her arms to her sides and let the oversize jacket slip to the floor. She took a small step toward him, her fingers unbuttoning the top button of the shirt she was wearing.

Days ago, she would have been afraid of this. She would have avoided it at all costs, just as she'd always avoided romantic entanglements. But recently the cost had become too high. She wanted to let herself live, explore, give, receive. If she had to pay the price with her heart, perhaps a broken heart, then so be it.

She realized that before she went any further, she owed him the truth, awkward and painful though it might be. "Bear," she said in a strained whisper, "I should warn you."

His gaze darkened, his senses alert to her every nuance. He hoped with all his might that she wasn't about to say good-bye.

"What?" he said, eager to end his misery one way or the other.

She swallowed thickly. "You know how you hadn't had much experience behind the wheel . . ."

He frowned. How could she be talking about his driving at a time like this? Then he saw her lower lip tremble slightly, and he sensed her turmoil. "Yes?" he prompted.

"Well, I happen to lack experience in . . . some areas myself."

He blinked once in what might have been surprise. Then his gaze softened, and he opened his arms. "Come here."

She moved into his embrace. There she felt complete and safe.

He touched her chin and gently lifted it so that he could look into her face. There was a smile in his eyes. "I'm not sure I'm qualified to be your driving instructor."

Her mouth curved with a wry twist at the corners. "There isn't anyone else I would rather have."

He gathered her close in his arms, feeling a deep tenderness he'd never known. He wanted to touch her so badly, his fingers ached, but he wanted more than anything to be patient with her, to give rather than take, to awaken her to the joy that loving could bring. He suspected there hadn't been enough joy in this woman's life.

Her heart was hammering against his chest as he stroked her hair. He let his fingers drift to her back where he drew lazy circles until he felt her relax, her muscles soften.

Slowly, he drew her a few inches away. While he brushed feather-weight kisses over her face, his fingers gently worked open the buttons of the shirt she was wearing.

When his fingers skimmed the swell of her breasts, her breath caught in her throat. His hands paused, then continued opening the buttons, one by one. He wanted to take his time, not just for her, but for himself too. He wanted to linger, to cherish, to luxuriate in the sensations he could bring to her.

He slipped the shirt from her shoulders and let it float to the floor. She was wearing a strapless wisp of lace that revealed more than it concealed. With the flick of his finger, he unhooked it and let it fall.

His lips traveled down her throat, pausing in the hollow where her pulse drummed. The clean scent of her filled his head. Her skin felt smooth and firm. He could feel her tremble slightly when he loosened the waistband of her jeans and slipped his fingers inside.

She stood still, her body pulsing with needs, her reticence holding her in check. Slowly, his fingers fanned out over her hips, guiding the rest of her clothes down until they dropped in a pool at her feet.

In that moment, while she stood facing him, naked, vulnerable, and trusting, he felt as though he was beginning an initiation of his own. He grasped her fingers and brought them to his lips.

He kissed her knuckles, turned her hands and kissed her palms and the inside of her wrists.

She threaded her fingers into his hair and drew him close, kissed his lips, and drew his head between her breasts. With a sigh she wrapped her arms around him, inviting him to explore. He let his tongue caress and play in languid circles until she gasped. He felt her tremble and caught her around the waist as she swayed unsteadily.

With one arm around her, he turned back the covers and guided her onto the bed. Swiftly, he pulled off his clothes to join her. When he reached for her, he discovered that his hands weren't steady. He forced himself to calm a bit. He couldn't let himself get carried away. He wanted to bring her pleasure first.

His fingers moved over her, soothing, sensitizing, and seducing. As he let them explore, he sent her emotions spiraling until she pressed against him, whispering his name. He aroused her skillfully, deliberately, and thoroughly.

Her body arched as sensations built in towering layers, driving her upward. He whispered to her reassuringly, lovingly. She was past listening, but his voice reached her in some far-off corner of her mind.

His lips moved over her skin, tasting, memorizing. She was calling his name in a desperate whisper that whipped his emotions into a frenzy. Driven by her total surrender, he levered himself above her. He entered her gently, knowing that his clearheaded control was soon to vanish. She tensed for a brief moment, then he began to move, slowly at first, until she joined him in the rhythm.

Breathlessly, she clung to him, her eyes half-closed until he drove her over the first peak. She gasped, and her eyes opened wide, filling with a look of wonder.

It was then that he let himself go with the cadence they both sought, ranging higher and higher until they both were floating in another realm.

Later, she lay spent beside him, feeling more than a little dazed. She curved herself around him, her head on his shoulder, her knee drawn up across his body. It felt right, lying here beside him, his arms and legs tangled with hers. She felt complete and whole. Here was the glow that poets had penned, artists had painted, musicians had played. Her eyelids closed, and she slept in his arms, dreaming contentedly.

The next morning she slipped from his bed and stepped into the shower. Moments later the glass door opened, and he stepped in beside her.

"Mind a little company?" he asked lazily, his eyes only halfway open.

She felt herself blushing to the hairline. Standing next to him naked, with sunlight streaming through the window high on the wall, seemed bolder than lying naked beside him in the night. "No," she managed to say in her husky morning voice.

The corners of his mouth lifted sympathetically. She was embarrassed and modest. He gathered her in his arms, knowing instinctively that she'd rather he held her than look at her. "Feeling okay?" he asked gently.

Her features softened. She was crazy about him, and it was hard not to show it. She didn't want him to think that she was such a ninny that because they'd made love, she was going to turn into some clinging vine all of a sudden. "More than okay, Malone."

He began to relax when he heard the sass in her voice. She would be all right now that she had her spunk back.

"And you?" she asked, with a hint of challenge in her voice.

"Well," he said, slowly rocking her in his arms under the shower spray. "I'm a little achy, and a whole lot tired, kinda stiff—"

"Yeah?" she interrupted with interest.

"You greedy child," he accused.

She wrapped her arms around his neck and drew his face down to hers. "I bet I'm not the only one."

He chuckled low. "I'll bet you're not."

An hour later, he struggled out of bed and pulled on his jeans. He glanced over his shoulder at her face on his pillow, her damp hair fanned out like a nimbus around her head, the sheet pulled up under her arms. He brushed a kiss on the tip of her nose. "I'll make us breakfast while you get dressed."

She nodded. He understood her reluctance to dress in front of him and was giving her some space. She needed a few more moments to collect herself. "Bye," she called softly as he padded out, closing the door behind him.

"Bye," he called as he marched down the stairs.

As she pulled on her clothes, she realized that she wasn't the same person she'd been the day before. She felt whole. She'd never thought another human being could give her that sense of completion. Somehow, she thought everything would be achieved through setting goals and working hard. This was a new thing for her. She stood for a few moments out on his balcony, watching the new day sparkle on the waves.

Somewhere along the way, she'd fallen in love with Bear Malone, and she knew in her heart that she'd never be the same. How that was going to change her life she wasn't sure. She did know that she wouldn't hang on to him, dragging him down. He'd made love with her, he'd opened a new world to her, but that didn't mean she would cast him chains. By the same token, she wasn't going to follow him around like a lovesick puppy.

He'd released her from her lifelong restraints. A part of her never wanted to leave his side, but the rest of her still cherished a measure of independence.

At work the following day, Christine was conferring with her secretary when Mr. Montgomery sent a message for her to meet with him as soon as possible.

Christine was ushered into his office minutes later. "Good morning. I understand you wish to see me, sir." At the arch of his brow, she added, "R.C."

"Have a seat." He gestured toward one of the plump leather wingback chairs opposite his large desk. Christine would have preferred to stand, or better yet, pace. Her nerves were jangling inside. It was rare for Montgomery to make an impromptu request like this, and she felt a certain uneasiness. She selected a chair and sat. "Coffee?" he asked.

"No, thank you." She tried to smile, but her face felt as though it had forgotten how.

He poured himself a cup and added a liberal

serving of creamer. A trickle of tension snaked down her spine when he chose to sit in the chair next to her instead of behind his desk.

He stirred his coffee in silence. Then he raised his eyes and locked onto her gaze. "Tell me, did you enjoy our party, Christine?"

She blinked. "Why, yes, of course."

"You left so early," he said matter-of-factly.

"I hope you weren't offended."

He leaned his head back on the thick cushion. "Actually, I was a bit puzzled. You didn't circulate much, and I wondered why. Yesterday I received a thank-you call from Mr. Mackey, whom you were visiting with most of the time."

"One of our advertising associates," she said with a nod, then she swallowed and waited.

"He seems quite impressed with you, as we all are." He paused for a beat. "However, the source of his enthusiasm is not ElectroFirst, as one would expect." His eyes narrowed a bit. "Strangely enough, it's some sort of volunteer project that you are leading."

"I've been arranging schedules for volunteers on a civic project," she confirmed.

He nodded slowly. "A key customer of ours was looking for you after you left."

"I regret that I missed him."

He took a sip and set his cup back in the saucer with an audible clink. "It could be said that you appear to have more dedication to the civic project than to ElectroFirst."

"I am dedicated to our company."

"I believe that you are, Christine. I feel that I've had a hand in nurturing your career. What we're discussing here is a matter of degree. While contributing to charity reflects well on our firm, it has come to my attention that you've used company time to solicit donations from some of our contacts."

Her lips parted a fraction. In her mind's eye, she saw Percy at the party, whispering into Montgomery's ear and gesturing toward her across the room. She cleared her throat and focused on the present. She tried to keep her voice low and even. The last thing she wanted to do was come off sounding defensive. "I believe the record will show that I work late here four nights out of five. The project I'm involved in takes nothing away from this company."

"I'm not criticizing you, Christine, but you must look at this from our point of view. I understand that sometimes at the end of business conversations with some of our vendors and outlets, you toss in a pitch for donations or discards. Now had you remained throughout the party, you could have spoken directly to those who mentioned the situation to me in passing. You could have reassured them that your heart is with ElectroFirst."

"I see." She was beginning to wonder if he would ever forgive her for leaving his party early. It had been only a party, after all. Or was that all it had been?

"I know you mean well," he said in a soothing tone. "But for someone as talented as you are, for someone with your potential, your career must come first. You see, when you're an excellent leader and you become involved in an extracurricular project, people often expect you to take an administrative role. True professionals rarely have the extra time that directing a project requires. Their energies are focused on their careers. It's one of the secrets of highly successful people.

Sometimes it becomes necessary to extricate your-self, Christine." He raised his brows and met her gaze directly. "Sometimes you have to just say no."

How original, she thought. But her heart was drumming in her ears. "You're suggesting I ease off for a while."

He set his cup and saucer on his desk. "I'm advising more than that, and if you're as wise as I think you are, you'll realize that my advice is usually stronger than a suggestion, Christine."

His message was coming through loud and clear, and it was back off or else.

Nine

On the following Thursday evening, Bear arrived early for the council's session to review the progress of their home-renewal project. He peeked inside the conference room. The mayor and the council members were already there getting organized.

Letting the door close, Bear began pacing up and down the hallway. He was too edgy to go inside yet. He hadn't heard from Christine all week. He'd expected her to drop by the house at least one evening to work or to check their progress or . . . at least, just to see him. After what they had shared together last weekend, he hadn't expected her to hide from him, but that's what it was beginning to look like to him.

No matter what time of day he tried to reach her at her apartment, he got her damned answering machine. He'd reluctantly called her at the office, but she had not responded to his messages there.

He walked to the front doors, and glanced up and down the street, searching for her little red car, cursing when it wasn't there. If she didn't show up at this meeting, he'd take a cab directly to her apartment, and he'd get inside one way or the other.

A wave of panic seized him, and his heart rate seemed to double. What if she'd been in an accident? Maybe she was lying in the wreckage of her automobile at this moment, comatose, unable to call for help? What if—

"Mr. Malone?" A voice behind him broke into his thoughts. "Bear?"

He wheeled around to face the mayor.

"We would like to begin even if Miss Brighton isn't here yet."

"I, uh, I'll be right along. . . ."

The mayor turned and headed back toward the conference room. Bear gave one last long look out the front doors before following the mayor down the hall.

Five minutes into the meeting, the wide conference room door swung open, and all eyes turned to greet Christine's arrival. Her face was flushed, and her hair was windblown. Her eyes darted around the table, pausing momentarily on Bear's face for just a second before she glanced away.

In that instant, in her quick look of dismissal, he knew that something was wrong. He didn't have to wait for her to choose an empty chair several places away from him. He stared at her for a moment. Maybe what had happened between them, the intimacy they had shared, the laughter, the loving, maybe that had simply added up to nothing more than a casual encounter for her.

Surely not, he told himself. How could a woman be so casual about her first lover? Certainly a woman who had waited until her midtwenties for her first love affair would not feel as uninvolved as Christine appeared to at that moment. Certainly not someone as sensitive and idealistic as Christine Brighton.

His heart sank. She looked so distant, so cool, so removed. Only that scarlet flush on her skin hinted that she might feel otherwise inside. Studying her, he noticed that her hands were shaking as she opened the folder in front of her.

The mayor clasped his hands on the table. "I'd like to repeat what I said at the beginning of the meeting and thank Bear and Christine for their wonderful contributions to our project." He clapped his hands, and the three councilmen joined him in giving the two of them a round of applause.

Looking embarrassed, Christine dropped her eyes to the folder before her.

The mayor shared his smile with the faces around the table. "We've known for some time that Bear is a master craftsman, but my, my, am I ever impressed with Christine's ability to solicit donations of every kind. Why, she even got one outfit to donate a delivery van." While the others nodded their approval, the mayor looked directly at Christine. "I want you to be the fund-raiser for my next election."

She looked down and shook her head slightly as if she didn't take him seriously.

"I'm serious, Christine," the mayor insisted. "I couldn't believe you got a load of concrete donated by old Jim Carsteen. To the best of my knowledge, he's never contributed anything to anybody. You must share your secret with us. How do you get so many people interested in our cause?"

She shifted in her chair and cleared her throat. "Through my job, I've had the opportunity to establish a relationship with vendors in the area."

Her voice seemed normal, but she avoided eye contact.

"Well, it beats all." The mayor nodded, opened his folder, and peered down through his bifocals. "Now, if you will all check your balance sheets, you'll see that we're still operating in the black, thanks to a federal grant and some generous patrons. Does anyone have any concerns about our finances that he or she would like to express at this time?"

No one spoke up. Bear kept an eye on Christine. He could sense her anxiety.

"Well, now," the mayor continued, looking at Christine, "with your fine recruiting skills supplying us volunteer crews, and, Bear, with your home-building skills as our foreman, I think we can wind up this project in, say, a few months?" He raised his silver brows and glanced from one to the other.

There was a long, silent moment before Bear finally said, "I think that sounds about right."

The mayor nodded his approval, and all eyes turned to Christine for her opinion.

Her glance flicked around the table, bouncing off the faces, carefully skipping over Bear before she dropped her gaze to the highly polished surface of the mahogany table. Taking a deep breath, she reached deep inside for all of the courage she could muster. "I, uh, need to talk with you about that." The room fell silent. "Lately, things have gotten hectic where I work, and I don't think . . . I can continue to cochair this project." There was an audible groan from the mayor, and Christine talked faster. "I still want to contribute some time. I'll pitch in whenever I can. It's just that I have to say that I don't think you should count on me to recruit manpower or solicit donations."

"Well," the mayor began in a stunned voice, "I

think I can speak for all of us in saying that we don't want to lose your leadership here. You've kept the project rolling at a steady pace. Why, we have such a winning combination that we'd hate to change a thing now."

The others chimed in and added similar sentiments—everyone but Bear who remained silent and subdued.

The mayor reached over to touch Christine's arm. "Feel free to slack back to a pace you can deal with for the time being. Surely, things will smooth out. They always do. We'll understand if you have to share some of the responsibility. Perhaps we can help out until you can see your way clear to—"

"Please," Christine interrupted, "I'd be less than honest if I let you believe that my problem is a temporary inconvenience. For the sake of the project, I suggest you find someone to replace me at this time."

"Because we know how much the project means to you," the mayor said, trying to console her, "we would consider only a temporary replacement, if we can find anyone at all. Going into the winter holidays, well, I just don't know that we can get someone to do what you've done so well."

Christine squeezed her eyes shut for a brief instant. "If and when my situation changes, I'll do what I can then, but you really should get someone right away."

The meeting broke up with an awkward silence. No one seemed to have anything to say. Christine gathered her things and wasted no time making her way to the parking lot.

Her heels were rapidly clicking across the pavement when a deep voice behind her brought her steps to a reluctant pause. "I wouldn't want to interrupt your busy schedule, but I do have a few unanswered questions."

Christine's heartbeat accelerated until it was throbbing in her ears. Deep down, she'd known she couldn't get away without talking to Bear one-on-one, but for a brief moment after she'd escaped the building and made her break for the car, she'd thought maybe she was home free. She slowly turned to face him. "I really must—" She stopped in midsentence as he cupped her elbow and whirled her around.

"We'll talk in your car," he said in a tight voice as he drew her to his side and steered her along.

She opened her mouth to protest but closed it when she realized how futile it was to resist. He wouldn't let her leave without a personal explanation. Unlocking her car, she glanced around the sparsely occupied parking lot. The last thing she wanted was to get into a public shouting match. She slipped behind the wheel and closed the door. During the few seconds it took him to walk around to the passenger side, she considered locking the doors and driving off, but she couldn't do that . . . not to the man she loved.

She stared out the window miserably. She'd known better than to get involved with someone she was working with so closely. She'd known better than to get involved with someone who was so different from herself. She'd known better, but still she'd cast wisdom and caution aside to fall headlong in love with Bear Malone.

When he dropped into the passenger seat beside her, she slid her arms over the steering wheel and slumped forward, plopping her forehead dejectedly on her hands. "I . . . I really would rather not talk about this now."

"No?" There was bitterness in his voice. "Since you won't answer my messages, I can't see that I have another option. Do you?"

She released a sigh. "I think we should wait till we can talk about it calmly."

"I'm calm."

She wanted to shriek that *she* was not calm, that she would never feel a moment's peace again now that she was hopelessly in love with a man who was going to hate her. "Let's not do this," she said in a whisper. She wanted to preserve the memory of those times in his arms and not tarnish it with harsh words.

It was as if he had not heard her protest. "First of all, I'd like to know why you're backing out on our project."

"I'm not backing out. I'm just—"

"No word games, Christine. You can save those for boys like Percy. I require straight answers."

"Okay." She pushed off the steering wheel to lean her head back against the headrest. "Things are heating up at work. The bottom line is I can't contribute the time . . . or the same resources to the project that I have in the past."

"So business at ElectroFirst is picking up that much?" The tone of his voice told her he wasn't buying a word of it.

"In a manner of speaking, yes."

"Is it me?" he asked in a tight voice. "Is it us?"

She could feel his eyes boring through her. She could feel the heat of accusation in his gaze. Finally, she forced herself to turn her head and make eye contact. She saw anger and frustration and something else that took her breath away.

Hurt, the hurt of rejection, searing and raw was in his eyes.

She knew what he was asking. He wanted to know if she was rejecting him or the project. If she was regretting the impetuous moment when she'd given in to towering emotions and made love with him, her only means of escape would be to quit the project. She reached out and touched his arm. His gaze riveted to hers, he ignored her gesture and waited for her reply.

"My decision to step down has nothing to do with us. It's purely business. I can stretch myself only so far." Her eyes pleaded with him for understanding, but his expression remained unchanged.

"Would you tell me . . . if you didn't want to see me anymore?" He was aware that his presence could be intimidating. Maybe she was trying to extricate herself in a manner that wouldn't anger him.

With a sinking heart, he realized that his behavior at this moment, practically kidnapping her in the parking lot, forcing the issue in her car, peppering her with hard-hitting questions would only validate any reason she might have for letting him down easy. He tore his gaze away. If that was the case, as he was beginning to believe it was, he would get real answers from her now. Actions speak louder than words, he reminded himself. If she loved him, she'd come to him. If she didn't, well, this was the moment to face the truth.

He'd never know for sure exactly when he had fallen in love with her. He shook his head at the irony. It could have been the first day she'd walked into the house for all he knew. All he knew for certain was that at some moment along the way, he'd lost his heart to this woman. With her, he'd run the full gamut of emotions: From suspicion, to resentment, to annoyance, to tolerance, to respect, to admiration, to affection, to passion . . . and to love.

As a leaden pain seeped into his heart, he wished he'd been able to shut off his feelings for her before he'd gotten in too deep. With a sigh, he admitted that it was too late for regrets.

"Bear, please, don't look so down." Her voice was a plaintive whisper. "Give me a little time to work things out."

He looked at her then, feeling that his worst fears were just confirmed. He could recognize a measure of pity in her voice as she let him down gently. The irony was that he could remember saying those exact words to others in his past.

The anger, the fight in him had disappeared. The kindness in her eyes had smothered it. He reached to cup her face in his hands one more time, maybe for the last time. Gently, he kissed her and managed to lift the corners of his mouth in a bittersweet smile.

"Take care, Christine." He swallowed around the lump in his throat and released her. Pulling the handle, he threw his shoulder against the door. Get out now, he told himself, before you make things worse.

"Bear . . ." She reached for him, but it was too late. He was standing outside, closing the door. "I'll be back."

"You'll know where to find me." With that, the door thudded closed, and he disappeared into the heavy mist that had crept in with the twilight.

She sat for a long moment, hating R. C. Montgomery, hating the ambition that had led her to this, hating herself for jeopardizing a future with the only man she'd ever loved. Where were her priorities? she wondered. Hot tears flowing down her cheeks, she slapped her palms helplessly against the steering wheel.

For the next few weeks, Christine devoted herself to ElectroFirst, arriving early, staying late. She still organized and scheduled work crews for the renewal project, but she made those phone calls from restaurant pay phones on her lunch breaks. She still solicited donations but not from any of the vendors or companies who did business with ElectroFirst.

A few times a week, she'd drive over to the house and work late at night alone, wallpapering rooms, painting inside trim, the final touches she'd longed to do from the beginning.

One evening she was working late at the house when she heard a key turn in the front door. She stepped into the dimly lit hallway, her heart thudding, violent scenes from movies she'd seen flashing into her mind.

Bear stepped inside and closed the door behind him. Her hand flew to her heart. "Oh, thank God, it's you."

"Were you expecting someone else?" His face was in shadows, and his voice was remote.

"I wasn't expecting anyone at all. That's what scared me."

"Sorry."

She wanted to run to him, throw her arms around him, tell him how much she'd missed him, how often she thought of him everyday. The chill in his voice and the way he wandered into the next room without a word squelched the urge. She left soon after that, realizing that it was too difficult to be that near to him and not have real closeness. The awkwardness between them was too much.

After that, she stopped going to the house, but a few days later, when she was on the phone with Sarah, the desire to know about Bear was too much to resist. "How is he?" she asked, certain that she wouldn't have to explain her actions or her curiosity to her friend.

"How do you think he is?" Sarah replied tartly. "Think you could see your way clear to join us once in a while?" Disapproval was evident in her voice.

"I don't know when I'll get free, Sarah."

"Well, think of us peons down there every now and then. Though I must say we're getting a lot done without you."

"Thanks. Nice to know I'm missed."

All trace of humor left Sarah's voice. "You are."

The next day, Christine received a call from Mr. Montgomery's personal assistant. "R.C. would like to see you in his office."

"I'll be right there," Christine returned politely, wondering about the nature of his summons.

Montgomery greeted her in a hearty tone and proceeded to tell her that he and "the boys in the home office" were quite impressed with her work of late.

"I knew I could count on you to make the right choices," he said, smiling broadly.

Christine dropped her gaze, thinking it unwise to let her boss see the irritation in her eyes that his remark was causing.

"I recognize leadership material when I see it,

and you, my dear, have what it takes." He paused dramatically. "Therefore, it gives me pleasure to inform you that general headquarters in New York wants you for an important position there."

Christine's eyes widened in surprise. "They do?"

Montgomery seemed pleased by her reaction. "Isn't that what every up-and-coming mid level executive dreams of?"

"I suppose so." Christine realized that her recent dreams had been filled with images of Bear Malone.

"I must say you don't seem as thrilled as I'd expected." The censure was clear in his voice. "Perhaps I should mention that your salary will increase by a third."

She glanced up. "It's just that I like it here. The thought of moving away bothers me."

He smiled warmly. "I can understand why you'd be reluctant to leave us. We've nurtured you, guided you, trained you, but it's time to leave the nest."

Two things dawned on her. Montgomery had assumed she was referring to the plant when she meant Santa Cruz. And he had not only offered her the promotion but had assumed her acceptance. How little he understood her.

Before she could explain, he continued, "You never know, Christine, perhaps you can move back here and take my job when I retire in another ten years or so."

Her heart sank. Ten years away from Santa Cruz sounded like a lifetime. "I'll need some time to think."

"Take all the time you need, but be packed and ready to go by the first." He chuckled. "That's a joke, Christine."

"Oh, yes, " she said, rising on unsteady legs. It was never easy to tell when Montgomery was making a joke. However, she was certain that he seriously intended for her to be winging her way to New York at the end of the year. She managed a wan smile as she shook his hand and excused herself from his office.

Some joke.

She spent the rest of the day behind her desk, staring out the window, too confused to do any work. It wasn't until her secretary popped her head in to say good night that she remembered she was seeing Bill Brosman that evening.

She arrived at Bernardo's before Bill. She selected a booth where she could keep an eye on the door, wondering what was so important that he'd called her a couple of days ago and insisted on this meeting.

Bill burst through the door at six-fifteen. He waved as he spotted Christine and made his way to her. They shook hands, exchanged welcoming smiles, and ordered wine.

"I'll get to the point, Christine. I had a chat with my accountants and my banker recently, and they seem to think that it's time for me to expand in another direction. So, I've got some change jingling in my pocket and a head full of ideas. Wondered if you'd hear me out?"

She nodded. "Sure."

"Well, my research tells me that the market is right to go into home renovating. There's only so much prime coastline real estate. People buy for location, then they often see that it's more cost productive to renovate than to bulldoze the existing structure and start from scratch. I don't have the time or the right people in place to head up a division like that, but I did think of you and Bear because a project like this takes special people, patient people to see the potential in a house and work with what's there. You already know how to train crews for this kind of work. I just think you and Bear make a heck of a team, you with your organizational skill, Bear with his home-building skills, and the attention to detail that you both give."

He raised his hand when she opened her mouth to speak. "Now, now, before you say anything, let me assure you that if you two want to work for me, you can still devote plenty of time to your pet project since you can set your own hours for both. I'm just asking you to think about it and get back to me."

"Have you spoken with Bear about this?"

"Not yet. Thought I'd sound it out with you first. With your steady career, I thought you'd stand the most to lose in trying it out. But let me assure you, Christine, the market is there. I can't tell you how many inquiries and referrals our construction company turns down in a year's time. We aren't set up to do that sort of thing at this time, and when Brosman Construction does something, it's done right. We don't wedge in a job and do it halfway. That's why I need you guys to make it work."

Christine could feel the adrenaline pumping through her as she imagined the possibilities. This was an opportunity that intrigued her. While she'd lacked enthusiasm for the ElectroFirst promotion, she felt excited by the prospect of heading up a division for Bill Brosman. And the idea of working with Bear, the hope of resolving their differences, the possibility of building something lasting with him sent her spirits soaring.

At the same time, a tingle of fear trickled down her spine. She'd be giving up a plum promotion to tackle the unknown with uncertain results.

"I will give it a lot of thought."

Bill nodded and smiled. "You think about it and see what you want to do, then talk to Bear if you'd like. You should know one thing, however."

Christine inclined her head attentively. "Yes?"

"I'd need you both to go with me on this, a package deal, so to speak."

"So to speak," she repeated. At this point, she didn't know whether Bear Malone was even speaking to her.

Ten

Slowly driving through the fog to the airport, Christine decided that her life was like the California weather, a long drought punctuated by a gush of rain. She was flying home for the holidays with her mind distracted by the choice of not one but two business opportunities after a long spell with none and her heart heavy with love for a man after having had no one special in her life.

Christine's father met her at the airport, and for a few days afterward she was spinning in the whirlwind of last-minute shopping and family get-togethers. On the afternoon that she was to leave, she and her mother were alone in the house, packing away the holiday decorations.

"Something is troubling you, Christine. I wonder if you're going to tell me what it is."

Christine's startled brown eyes lifted to meet her mother's serene gaze, then she released her breath in a whoosh. She hadn't known how to begin, but as she had so many times before, her mother made it easy for her. "Decisions, decisions. I think I'm going out of my mind."

Her mother's mouth curved. "Business?"

She nodded and proceeded to tell her about the promotion and Bill's proposal, finishing with the most important detail. Bill wants a package deal. Bear Malone and I must agree to head up the new division together.

"Could you work with this . . . Bear?"

"I could marry him, Mother." The admission didn't startle Christine one bit. She smiled, remembering her run-ins with Bear from the beginning. Before she knew it, she had spilled out the events that had characterized their relationship.

"Sounds like he means a lot to you."

"Too much," Christine replied in a whisper.

"Too much?"

"I don't know that I want to get myself into a situation where I lose my identity, lose my freedom, lose sight of who I am." Christine's voice grew stronger as the words tumbled out. "I would hate living under someone else's thumb."

"The way you think I've lived under your father's thumb?"

Christine's eyes flew to her mother's face. What she found was the astute patience she'd encountered there before, but this time she recognized the wisdom.

"Well, I uh . . . I suppose I've always thought you gave up everything for Dad and me." The last thing she wanted to do was hurt her mother's feelings, but perhaps it was time to get it out into the open. She sighed and dropped her gaze to her hands. "It seemed to me that you never had a life of your own, time for your own dreams, your own accomplishments."

"You're mistaken about that," her mother said quietly. "My dream for as long as I can remember was to have a successful marriage, a loving husband, and a well-adjusted child who'd grow into a happy adult."

"Guess I let you down on the last one."

Her mother smiled gently. "I don't think so, but I do want to see you happy. Didn't I permit you to make your own choices?"

"Yes, since I was small."

Her mother put the table arrangement she'd wrapped aside. "Then why can't you allow that I've made my choices, followed my dreams, achieved what I wanted to accomplish?"

Christine blinked hard and shrugged. "I . . . I don't know. I guess I just assumed—"

"Assumed that because I was home instead of crisscrossing the country in a power suit with an attaché stuck under my arm that I couldn't possibly be fulfilled?" her mother demanded with her brows arched indignantly.

Christine chuckled at the image her mother had painted. "That wouldn't be you, Mom."

"My point exactly."

"I'm sorry. Jumping to conclusions like that wasn't fair to you."

"Apology accepted." Her mother's eyes warmed. "Now that we have my life understood, what are we going to do about yours?"

Christine shook her head. "You haven't heard the worst of it."

"Why don't you fill me in."

"I really do think I'm madly in love with Bear Malone, and he thinks I'm a power-hungry yuppie out for riches and fame."

"If Bear is the kind of man you described before, I think he would know you better than that by now."

Christine thought of the intimate moments they'd spent together and nodded slowly. "You're right. But all that changed when I stepped down from leading the project. He suspects that my job had something to do with it, but that doesn't make sense to him. He probably thinks I should quit my job and work full-time on the project like he does."

"Is that such a bad idea?"

"Mom, it's a great idea, for people like him who have an independent income. Shoot, I have monthly expenses, college loans to pay back. I can't walk away from a good salary just like that."

"You can renegotiate your college loans and find ways to reduce your other expenses. And your father and I can always help out."

Christine smiled. "You're right as always, and thanks for the offer. But I'm sure I'll manage on my own. Call it stubbornness, but it means a lot to me to do this by myself." She gazed out the window at the snow falling in big flakes.

"What else is troubling you, dear?"

"It's Bear. I care so much about him, and he has such a low opinion of me. It hurts."

"It sounds like you two might have gotten off to a bad start, but I don't think he could spend that much time with my daughter without realizing that she's quality through and through."

"You're biased."

Her mother shrugged. "Maybe."

"Well, I'm glad that you are. It's just so scary. Whatever choices I make now will change my life . . . forever."

"Then do what I did. Follow your heart. Find what it is that fires your imagination, that boosts your energy, that brings you bliss, and then choose whatever that is. You can hardly go wrong."

Christine's eyes warmed. "Good advice, Mom." She had wasted precious time misjudging her mother, and she could see that she was doing the same thing again by misjudging the man she loved. It was time to set the record straight.

Her mother looked deeply into Christine's eyes. "Let me know how everything turns out."

"I will, Mom. And thanks."

When she got back to Santa Cruz, her first stop was the neighborhood service station. For what had to be the millionth time, the station manager leaned over the counter and asked her, "Tell me, when you gonna sell me that hot little car, huh?" His face split into an engaging grin. It had become a game with him, and he looked prepared for her usual refusal.

This time she cocked her head and looked at him. "What would you offer me for it?"

"Well—" he began, then paused before continuing, "you can't be serious?"

She lifted her shoulders. "Try me. It's my pride and joy, but you could make a generous offer, promise to take good care of it and give it a good home, and, who knows, we might be able to do business."

His eyes widened, and he hustled around the counter to take her elbow. On the way to the door he called out over his shoulder, "Take over, Jimmy. I'm busy."

After some tough negotiating, Christine drove out of the service station with a sizable check in her pocket but without her BMW. She was behind the wheel of an old minivan that the manager had thrown in as a trade. He'd insisted that it was reliable, in spite of the hundred thousand plus on the speedometer. It certainly wasn't a performance vehicle, but it would do for now. She figured after she paid off her car loan, she'd have a little nest egg to tide her over.

She drove home, unpacked her luggage, and changed into jeans. Her phone messages included several calls from the volunteers, asking her to return their calls immediately, but there was no message from the one person she'd most hoped would have called.

She glanced around her apartment, seeing it with new eyes, noticing how it lacked personal touches. Decorating it was something she'd always thought she'd get around to, but she had used her apartment only to sleep, bathe, and change in.

She stared at the phone. More than anything she wanted to see Bear, and if she called him, she could speak to him right away. She had missed him so much that she gave in to the temptation of a quick call.

She tapped her toe as she listened to his phone ring ten long times. Sighing, she finally hung up. It shouldn't surprise her, she decided, that he didn't have an answering machine.

Feeling too restless to stay in her apartment another minute, she decided to take a drive. Perhaps she'd stop by Bear's beach home or pop in at the house to see how it was coming along. She was tired, but too tired to sleep.

A restless energy possessed her, a restlessness borne of going too long without rest, a restlessness borne of deliberating too long over choices, fretting too long over outcomes. She was to the point where she'd prefer to make an impulsive decision than to remain suspended by indecision.

She hopped into the old van and started driving. Out of habit, she drove by ElectroFirst. The plant was virtually empty on Saturday night. Without the activity of trucks, cars, and people, it looked sterile and drab. For the first time, she was seeing it with an objective eye. In the evening mist, it seemed a sad place to spend the best days of one's life, closed off from the outside world. She realized that she was looking not at her future, but at her past.

On impulse, she drove to Bear's beach home. She walked to the door, knowing before she knocked that he wasn't there. Wherever he was, there was always life, noise, energy, and vitality. His home looked empty and dark without his presence, the same way she felt without him in her life. She glanced at her watch. He should be home by now. She shrugged in the chill of the deepening twilight. Perhaps he was still working at the house, she decided, as she turned toward the van.

Her eyes widened as she pulled up in front of the house. The driveway and street were full of cars. People were standing on the front porch, and every light was on in every room. It looked as though a party was just getting into full swing.

She couldn't have driven away if she'd wanted to. Curiosity was too strong. By the time she reached the front porch, she could smell the aroma of burgers sizzling on the grill and chili simmering on the stove.

She recognized volunteers from the work crews and local contributors. Inside the mayor took her jacket. "Welcome, Christine. I can't stress what a debt of gratitude we owe you for the completion of this house. It will soon be home for a lucky family of five."

"That's great," she replied as he pumped her hand.

"Help yourself to the refreshments," he said, as he turned to greet a couple behind her.

She found Sarah in the kitchen. "I didn't know there was going to be a party."

"A last-minute brainstorm. I left messages on your machine every day when I called." She shrugged. "I didn't know how to reach you in Iowa."

"It's okay," Christine responded. Then, unable to wait through polite conversation to get to the important question, she asked, "Where's Bear?"

Sarah smiled knowingly. "He drove down to the corner market for more hot dogs."

Christine did a double take. "Did you say he drove?"

Sarah nodded as though it was no big deal.

"Who went with him?" Christine asked casually, wondering if Bear had brought a date to the party.

"He went by himself."

"Someone should have gone with him. What if he gets pulled over? They'll ticket him for driving without a—"

"You don't have to quote the law to me," Sarah said, looking at her drolly. "Besides, Bear got his license last week."

"Oh." Christine dropped her head, feeling the wind go out of her sails.

"You haven't dropped by for a while." Sarah looked at her friend quizzically.

"I've missed you all." Christine looked wistfully at the shiny new windows and freshly painted shutters. "Guess I missed a lot around here."

"You could say that. We finished the house, planned a party, Bear got his license and bought a car."

"A car? Bear Malone bought a car?" She couldn't believe that Sarah meant Bear.

"He's a legal driver. Why shouldn't he own a car?"

Christine shook her head. "I have been away too long."

Sarah patted her back soothingly.

Christine looked her friend in the eye. "You have to tell me something before he gets back."

"Ask away." Sarah grinned impishly. "I might tell, then again I might not."

"Oh, you'll tell all right." Christine playfully grabbed a handful of Sarah's short dark locks. "Did Bear bring a date to this party?"

Sarah looked at her friend's dark frown. "I won't torture you. No, he didn't."

"Has he seemed . . . happy lately?" Christine asked, wondering if Bear was feeling as jubilant as the rest of the crowd here, wondering if he'd even thought about her or missed her at all.

Sarah shook her head. "A good attorney knows when to keep her mouth shut. You won't find me repeating hearsay. I suggest that you drive over to the market and see for yourself."

Christine straightened her shoulders. "Don't mind if I do."

A few minutes later, she pulled up to the door at the corner market. It would soon be closing, so there were only a half-dozen cars parked nearby. She scanned them, trying to pick out the one that Bear would have chosen. She drew a blank.

At that moment, she heard the doors slide and she glanced up to see Bear Malone step outside.

The sight of him nearly stole her breath away. She'd missed him even more than she'd thought. He looked so handsome in his slim jeans and bright red sweater. She wanted to leap out and hug him, but she sat transfixed, staring.

He glanced at her out of the corner of his eye as he walked right past her door and turned his back to set a sack of groceries on the passenger seat of the black convertible roadster parked next to her. He was close enough for her to reach through her open window and touch his back, but her hands lay clutched together on her lap. For an instant, he froze, then turned around slowly to peer into her window. "Christine?"

She nodded. "Yes."

He looked stunned. "I didn't expect to see you here." His gaze wandered over the plain brown minivan. "And certainly not in that." His brows knit together. "Your car in the shop?"

"This is my car . . . now."

He looked at her in disbelief. "You wrecked your BMW?"

She shook her head. "I sold it. Traded it, actually, for this one."

He chuckled. "This just isn't you, Christine."

"It'll do for now." Her eyes left his face to glance down over his sporty black two-seater. "And what's this?"

"Oh, uh . . . I bought it after I got my license last week." He looked flustered and embarrassed.

"Very nice."

"A good buy," he added, defensively.

The corners of her mouth lifted. "And so practical too." There were two little seats, a rag top, and a trunk that would hardly hold his toolbox, much less a suitcase.

He shrugged. "I guess you figured I'd buy something, well, dull and practical."

"Like this?" Christine patted the cracked steering wheel of her well-traveled minivan. "Experienced, I think the previous owner called it."

"Yeah, something like that."

"Actually, I'm a little surprised you bought a car at all, but I don't see why you shouldn't." Her brows arched, and a teasing light entered her eyes. "So what if people accuse you of driving a yuppie mobile. Drive what you like. I always do."

He glanced at his snazzy roadster. "Actually, I think this car reminded me of you."

"Oh, thanks," she said in a dry tone.

"No, really," he began earnestly. "It made me think of how you looked driving down the street, the wind tossing your hair around your face. I know it wasn't a practical choice, but at the time I couldn't resist." They both chuckled at the irony of it. "Well," Bear concluded, "we're a real pair, aren't we?"

Their eyes met, and the evening grew quiet around them. "Are we?" Christine asked finally.

Bear looked at the ground and back at her, then shrugged. "There's a party down the street. Would you like to join me there?"

She nodded. "I'd really like that."

He smiled warmly. It was a start. A bubble of hope lifted off inside her. "Lead the way."

She followed and parked behind him. It was hard to imagine him driving his own car. She remembered his first lesson behind the wheel in the cemetery. So much had changed.

He tucked the grocery bag under his arm and opened the door of her van. As he helped her out, he took her hand in his. Crossing the lawn, he squeezed her hand and straightened his arm, drawing her close to his side. She wondered if he still had strong feelings for her as they walked inside the house that together they had managed to transform.

While they'd been gone, Bill Brosman had arrived. He hurried over to them as Bear handed the sack of groceries over to Sarah. "Boy, am I glad to see you two," he began.

Christine crossed her fingers, hoping that Bill would omit any discussion of his business offer. One thing at a time, she thought, trying to send him a silent message with her eyes.

"Given any thought to our little enterprise?"

Bear looked at him blankly. "And what would that be?"

Christine's heart gave a little lurch. So much for mental telepathy, she thought to herself.

Bill looked incredulous. "Hasn't Christine told you?"

She looked at Bill pointedly. "I just got back from Iowa, Bill. We haven't had time to talk yet."

Bill's expression turned sheepish. He'd jumped the gun, and now he realized it. "Oh," he stammered, "well, there's no rush. I just thought . . ." He clapped Bear's shoulder. "We'll make a heck of a team. A package deal." He chuckled nervously, aware from their faces that he was making matters worse. "Well, gotta shove off now. Get back to me sometime."

Bill was grabbing his jacket off a peg and heading for the door when Bear turned to her. "What did he mean by all that?"

"Could we talk . . . privately?"

Bear grabbed a couple of beers, handed her one, and led the way to the backyard. He gestured to a wooden bench that he'd made, and she sat down. "Care for something to eat?" he asked.

"No, thanks." She felt too edgy to eat.

"So," he began, taking a seat a few feet from her, "what's the deal with Brosman?"

"I wish he hadn't said anything. I'd rather just celebrate the completion of this project. The house turned out great. You really did a good job."

"Thank you." He studied her in the starlight. "Why are you avoiding the subject Brosman raised?"

She sighed. Bear wouldn't be satisfied until she told him the details, so she proceeded to fill him in. He listened quietly, his expression passive. "Let me see if I've got this right," he replied when she'd finished. "He wants both of us."

"Yes."

"Is that what he meant by a package deal?" There was a wariness in his voice. "It has to be both of us, or no dice?"

She nodded. "That's the impression I got."

"I see." He tipped his head back and stared at the cluster of stars overhead. "So you waltz back over here and look me up to round out a nice business opportunity."

"There's more to it than that."

His head swung down, and he looked at her directly. "Not enough, I'm afraid."

He'd hoped and prayed for weeks that she would come back to him. When he'd seen her outside the market, his heart had jumped into his throat. He'd thought she'd come back to him, and he'd let himself believe that everything was going to be all right. He'd been giddy with joy at his good fortune. Now he felt nothing but disappointment. She'd come back to him all right to clinch a sweet business deal.

A panicky look crossed her face. "Bear, don't be like that. Whatever you want to do about Brosman's offer is your decision. For what it's worth, I came here tonight to see you."

"Right," he said with a tinge of bitterness. "Well, sweetheart, no need to sleep on it. I can give you my answer now. Count me out."

He was on his feet, heading for the house. Christine sat there feeling stricken. Bad timing as usual, she thought morosely. She dropped her head in her hands. If things had been different, she thought. If only Brosman had kept his mouth shut. She shook her head. It probably wouldn't have made any difference. Try though they might, it seemed that she and Bear were always at cross purposes.

She couldn't face the party, not with a tear-stained face and a broken heart. She walked around the side of the house out to the street. She'd just climbed in her minivan and shut the door, when she heard a knock on the window on the passenger side. "Who is it?"

"Brosman," came the reply. "Can I talk to you a minute?"

She unlocked the passenger door, and Bill Brosman crawled into the seat. "How'd it go after I left?" he asked nervously.

She shook her head. "Bear is not interested in the deal."

"I'm sorry if I spoiled things. I felt sure this would be perfect for you two. Maybe if I reassure him that—"

"I'm afraid his refusal has more to do with me than you. I'm afraid a package deal with Bear and me is out of the question. You might get him if you drop me, but due to his personal objections toward me"—her voice cracked and her eyes filled—"I'm afraid you'll have to make other arrangements."

"Are you willing to quit your job and head up my division?" he asked briskly.

Christine thought for a moment. It looked as though she couldn't have it all, but she'd made up her mind that she wasn't going back to Electro-First at any rate. She nodded slowly. "Yes."

"Then the position is yours. I would still like to have Bear if he changes his mind. Do you think it would help if I talked with Bear myself?" he asked gently.

"The truth?" she asked, and he nodded. "I think it would make it worse."

He patted her shoulder. "Sorry, kid. I didn't mean to foul things up."

"Don't blame yourself, Bill. People who work together have to respect each other, trust each other. Better to know that now."

But her heart didn't believe it.

She gave her two weeks' notice to ElectroFirst. Montgomery was so disgusted with her that he applied her leftover vacation time and released her after a week. It had been a long time since she'd had a few days to do anything she wanted.

She went to the beach. It felt good to trudge through the sand and feel the sea breeze whipping her hair. The gulls screeched overhead, and she inhaled the salty air. She stooped to gather bits of litter, tossing them into barrels along the way. Occasionally, she glanced at the clifftop homes and beach houses, wondering if the people who lived in them were happy or heartbroken.

When her legs began to cramp, she stopped to catch her breath and gaze around. Just ahead, she saw Bear's beach home. Her heart began to thud when she spotted him sitting in a deck chair.

It occurred to her that this had been her destination all along, consciously or unconsciously, she wasn't sure. She couldn't tell if he had seen her or not. A part of her wanted to turn and run, but she wouldn't permit it. In the last month, she'd changed her life for the better by giving up some things and accepting some risks. Perhaps it was time to toss aside her pride and face the big risk, the one where she stood the most to lose.

As she slowly walked toward him, her eyes locked with his. He looked so tired, so beaten. She stopped at the edge of his deck, and they stared into each other's eyes for a long moment. Finally, Christine knocked on the wooden railing. "Hello, anybody home?"

"Who's there?" he asked in a quiet voice.

She raised a plastic wineglass she'd found on the beach. "Just a neighbor, come to borrow a cup of anything . . . you might be willing to give."

"Oh, I think we can do better than that." He rose from his chair and held out his hand.

Her eyes filled with tears as she placed her hand in his. He pulled her onto the porch and into his arms. They held each other tightly as tears flowed down her cheeks.

He took her inside and reached under her chin to tilt her face up to his. "I've missed you so much, Christine," he whispered. "My life is hell without you."

"Mine too. There are some things I need to tell you."

He nodded. "Me too."

She swallowed her fear and plunged on. "I happen to love you, Bear Malone. No matter what you think of me, I love you."

His eyes softened, and a smile touched his lips. "I love you too, Christine."

"You do?"

To prove it, he took her lips in a heated, tumultuous kiss. When he pulled back a long moment later, he gazed lovingly into her eyes. "For the past two hours, I've been telling that damn answering machine of yours how much I love you and what a fool I was the other night. I had such high hopes for us, and I jumped to conclusions again. I'm sorry. I was wrong. There wasn't anything wrong with his offer. I just wanted to believe that you came back for me." His voice grew impatient. "Don't you check your messages?"

"Not lately," she said, wrapping her arms around his neck, "but you can be sure I'll play those messages back over and over again."

"You won't need to because I'll repeat them until you get tired of hearing them."

"That'll be the day. I think I could hear you tell me that you love me every day of my life, and I'd never tire of hearing it."

He looked deeply into her eyes. "If I have my way, we'll test your theory."

"That so?" she prompted, nuzzling his throat.

He lifted her chin so that she met his gaze. "The other night you asked me to be your business partner. I've given that a lot of thought." When she began to protest, he covered her mouth. "Shhh, let me counter that offer." Her brows rose. "I want you to be my partner for life as well. I'm asking you to marry me, Christine. What do you say?"

Her face flushed with joy. "Yes, yes." She hugged him tightly.

He pulled her back, and his look was intense. "We'll make a partnership built to last . . . on respect, on trust, on love."

She smiled into his eyes. "Deal."

He chuckled deep and full. "Tell Brosman he can have his package deal, if his offer still stands," he managed to say before she crushed his mouth to hers.

Deal or no deal, Christine knew she had what she wanted. For the rest of her life.

THE EDITOR'S CORNER

There's a lot to look forward to from LOVESWEPT in October—five fabulous stories from your favorites, and a delightful novel from an exciting new author. You know you can always rely on LOVESWEPT to provide six top-notch—and thrilling—romances each and every month.

Leading the lineup is Marcia Evanick, with **SWEET TEMPTATION,** LOVESWEPT #570. And sweet temptation is just what Augusta Bodine is, as Garrison Fisher soon finds out. Paleontologist Garrison thinks the Georgia peach can't survive roughing it in his dusty dinosaur-fossil dig—but she meets his skepticism with bewitching stubbornness and a wildfire taste for adventure that he quickly longs to explore . . . and satisfy. Marcia is at her best with this heartwarming and funny romance.

Strange occurrences and the magic of love are waiting for you on board the **SCARLET BUTTERFLY,** LOVESWEPT #571, by Sandra Chastain. Ever since Sean Rogan restored the ancient—and possibly haunted—ship, he'd been prepared for anything, except the woman he finds sleeping in his bunk! The rogue sea captain warns Carolina Evans that he's no safe haven in a storm, but she's intent on fulfilling a promise made long ago, a promise of love. Boldly imaginative, richly emotional, **SCARLET BUTTERFLY** is a winner from Sandra.

Please give a big welcome to new author Leanne Banks and her very first LOVESWEPT, **GUARDIAN ANGEL,** #572. In this enchanting romance Talia McKenzie is caught in the impossible situation of working very closely with Trace Barringer on a charity drive. He'd starred in her teenage daydreams, but now there's bad blood between their families. What is she to do, especially when Trace wants nothing less from her than her love? The answer makes for one surefire treat. Enjoy one of our New Faces of 1992!

Ever-popular Fayrene Preston creates a blazing inferno of desire in **IN THE HEAT OF THE NIGHT,** LOVESWEPT #573. Philip Killane expects trouble when Jacey finally comes home after so many years, for he's never forgotten the night she'd branded him with her fire, the night that had nearly ruined their lives. But he isn't prepared for the fact that his stepsister is more gorgeous than ever . . . or that he wants a second chance. An utterly sensational romance, with passion at its most potent—only from Fayrene!

In Gail Douglas's new LOVESWEPT, **THE LADY IS A SCAMP,** #574, the lady in the title is event planner Victoria Chase. She's usually poised and elegant, but businessman Dan Stewart upsets her equilibrium. Maybe it's his handshake that sets her on fire, or the intense blue eyes that see right inside her soul. She should be running to the hills instead of straight into his arms. This story showcases the winning charm of Gail's writing—plus a puppet and a clown who show our hero and heroine the path to love.

We end the month with **FORBIDDEN DREAMS** by Judy Gill, LOVESWEPT #575. When Jason O'Keefe blows back into Shell Landry's life with all the force of the winter storm howling outside her isolated cabin, they become trapped together in a cocoon of pleasure. Jason needs her to expose a con artist, and he also needs her kisses. Shell wants to trust him, but so much is at stake, including the secret that had finally brought her peace. Judy will leave you breathless with the elemental force raging between these two people.

On sale this month from FANFARE are three exciting novels. In **DAWN ON A JADE SEA** Jessica Bryan, the award-winning author of **ACROSS A WINE-DARK SEA,** once more intertwines romance, fantasy, and ancient history to create an utterly spellbinding story. Set against the stunning pageantry of ancient China, **DAWN ON A JADE SEA** brings together Rhea, a merperson from an undersea world, and Red Tiger, a son of merchants who has vowed revenge against the powerful nobleman who destroyed his family.

Now's your chance to grab a copy of **BLAZE,** by bestselling author Susan Johnson, and read the novel that won the *Romantic Times* award for Best Sensual Historical Romance and a Golden Certificate from *Affaire de Coeur* "for the quality, excellence of writing, entertainment and enjoyment it gave the readers." In this sizzling novel a Boston heiress is swept into a storm of passion she's never imagined, held spellbound by an Absarokee Indian who knows every woman's desires. . . .

Anytime we publish a book by Iris Johansen, it's an event—and **LAST BRIDGE HOME** shows why. Original, emotional, and sensual, it's romantic suspense at its most compelling. It begins with Jon Sandell, a man with many secrets and one remarkable power, appearing at Elizabeth Ramsey's cottage. When he reveals that he's there to protect her from danger, Elizabeth doesn't know whether this mesmerizing stranger is friend or foe. . . .

Also on sale this month in the Doubleday hardcover edition is **LADY DEFIANT** by Suzanne Robinson, a thrilling historical romance that brings back Blade, who was introduced in **LADY GALLANT.** Now Blade is one of Queen Elizabeth's most dangerous spies, and he must romance a beauty named Oriel who holds a clue that could alter the course of history.

Happy reading!

With warmest wishes,

Nita Taublib

Nita Taublib
Associate Publisher
LOVESWEPT and FANFARE

OFFICIAL RULES TO WINNERS CLASSIC SWEEPSTAKES

No Purchase necessary. To enter the sweepstakes follow instructions found elsewhere in this offer. You can also enter the sweepstakes by hand printing your name, address, city, state and zip code on a 3" x 5" piece of paper and mailing it to: Winners Classic Sweepstakes, P.O. Box 785, Gibbstown, NJ 08027. Mail each entry separately. Sweepstakes begins 12/1/91. Entries must be received by 6/1/93. Some presentations of this sweepstakes may feature a deadline for the Early Bird prize. If the offer you receive does, then to be eligible for the Early Bird prize your entry must be received according to the Early Bird date specified. Not responsible for lost, late, damaged, misdirected, illegible or postage due mail. Mechanically reproduced entries are not eligible. All entries become property of the sponsor and will not be returned.

Prize Selection/Validations: Winners will be selected in random drawings on or about 7/30/93, by VENTURA ASSOCIATES, INC., an independent judging organization whose decisions are final. Odds of winning are determined by total number of entries received. Circulation of this sweepstakes is estimated not to exceed 200 million. Entrants need not be present to win. All prizes are guaranteed to be awarded and delivered to winners. Winners will be notified by mail and may be required to complete an affidavit of eligibility and release of liability which must be returned within 14 days of date of notification or alternate winners will be selected. Any guest of a trip winner will also be required to execute a release of liability. Any prize notification letter or any prize returned to a participating sponsor, Bantam Doubleday Dell Publishing Group, Inc., its participating divisions or subsidiaries, or VENTURA ASSOCIATES, INC. as undeliverable will be awarded to an alternate winner. Prizes are not transferable. No multiple prize winners except as may be necessary due to unavailability, in which case a prize of equal or greater value will be awarded. Prizes will be awarded approximately 90 days after the drawing. All taxes, automobile license and registration fees, if applicable, are the sole responsibility of the winners. Entry constitutes permission (except where prohibited) to use winners' names and likenesses for publicity purposes without further or other compensation.

Participation: This sweepstakes is open to residents of the United States and Canada, except for the province of Quebec. This sweepstakes is sponsored by Bantam Doubleday Dell Publishing Group, Inc. (BDD), 666 Fifth Avenue, New York, NY 10103. Versions of this sweepstakes with different graphics will be offered in conjunction with various solicitations or promotions by different subsidiaries and divisions of BDD. Employees and their families of BDD, its division, subsidiaries, advertising agencies, and VENTURA ASSOCIATES, INC., are not eligible.

Canadian residents, in order to win, must first correctly answer a time limited arithmetical skill testing question. Void in Quebec and wherever prohibited or restricted by law. Subject to all federal, state, local and provincial laws and regulations.

Prizes: The following values for prizes are determined by the manufacturers' suggested retail prices or by what these items are currently known to be selling for at the time this offer was published. Approximate retail values include handling and delivery of prizes. Estimated maximum retail value of prizes: 1 Grand Prize ($27,500 if merchandise or $25,000 Cash); 1 First Prize ($3,000); 5 Second Prizes ($400 each); 35 Third Prizes ($100 each); 1,000 Fourth Prizes ($9.00 each) ; 1 Early Bird Prize ($5,000); Total approximate maximum retail value is $50,000. Winners will have the option of selecting any prize offered at level won. Automobile winner must have a valid driver's license at the time the car is awarded. Trips are subject to space and departure availability. Certain black-out dates may apply. Travel must be completed within one year from the time the prize is awarded. Minors must be accompanied by an adult. Prizes won by minors will be awarded in the name of parent or legal guardian.

For a list of Major Prize Winners (available after 7/30/93): send a self-addressed, stamped envelope entirely separate from your entry to: Winners Classic Sweepstakes Winners, P.O. Box 825, Gibbstown, NJ 08027. Requests must be received by 6/1/93. DO NOT SEND ANY OTHER CORRESPONDENCE TO THIS P.O. BOX.

FANFARE

On Sale in August

DAWN ON A JADE SEA

☐ 29837-2 $5.50/6.50 in Canada
by Jessica Bryan

bestselling author of ACROSS A WINE-DARK SEA

She was a shimmering beauty from a kingdom of legend. A vision had brought Rhea to the glorious city of Ch'ang-an, compelling her to seek a green-eyed, auburn-haired foreign warrior called Zhao, the Red Tiger. Amid the jasmine of the Imperial Garden, passion will be born, hot as fire, strong as steel, eternal as the ocean tides.

BLAZE

☐ 29957-3 $5.50/6.50 in Canada
by Susan Johnson

bestselling author of FORBIDDEN and SINFUL

To Blaze Braddock, beautiful, pampered daughter of a millionaire, the American gold rush was a chance to flee the stifling codes of Boston society. But when Jon Hazard Black, a proud young Absarokee chief, challenged her father's land claim, Blaze was swept up in a storm of passions she had never before even imagined.

LAST BRIDGE HOME

☐ 29871-2 $4.50/5.50 in Canada
by Iris Johansen

bestselling author of THE GOLDEN BARBARIAN

Jon Sandell is a man with many secrets and one remarkable power, the ability to read a woman's mind, to touch her soul, to know her every waking desire. His vital mission is to rescue a woman unaware of the danger she is in. But who will protect her from him?

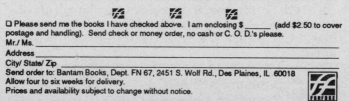